Essence of
Love

Essence of Love

Donald J. Porter

Writers Club Press
San Jose New York Lincoln Shanghai

Essence of Love

Writers Club Press
an imprint of iUniverse.com, Inc.

For information address:
iUniverse.com, Inc.
5220 S 16th, Ste. 200
Lincoln, NE 68512
www.iuniverse.com

ISBN: 0-595-00211-0

Printed in the United States of America

CHAPTER ONE

The Lake Shore Limited train raced through the vineyards of western New York state and the horrible, tragic thoughts raced through his brain. Tom had planned this eight thousand mile journey to get away, to forget, to be alone with his thoughts, and to start building a new life. Perhaps it would be successful. He was in the process of putting the past into the recesses of his mind. But there would always be some flashes of memory. Still there, faintly recalled, would be his love of forty–two years. He thought of the line of an unknown writer who penned: "The past never expires. It is always there to be remembered." She was gone. Death is the ultimate in finality.

The track curved to the south allowing the setting sun to bring him out of his reverie. The vivid rays were an inviolable force that made him, again, look out the window. The thought of death was gone, replaced by unsurpassed beauty outside. The thick, billowing clouds framing the edges of the window were softened by wispy traces of cirrus. And the colors, the ethereal colors, radiating from the half set sun were too beautiful to be painted—even by Monet or Cezanne.

The orange color, solid at the center, diffused into rays of misty lighter orange, then into soft marigold yellow, and suddenly red. Flecks of scarlet interspersed the veil–like clouds, and dappled the small amount of blue left in the sky. But the colors changed almost constantly and quickly. Suddenly, so small it could easily be missed, a fleeting touch of green showed itself at the top of the nearly set sun. It was breath–taking in its beauty. Then, as if the final curtain had been drawn, it all faded and disappeared. The sky was dark.

He recalled the words of Teddy Roosevelt—"To adequately describe it would bankrupt the English language".

The Journey had now brought him to Cleveland, Ohio on the shore of Lake Erie. Tom's train wouldn't chug out of the station for two more hours, so he decided to take a walk.

Across the street from the train station he saw a park. He threaded his way through the traffic to the oasis of beauty and tranquility. Huge trees flung their branches over old, winding brick paths. Row upon row of multi–colored tulips surged up a gentle slope of hill, like ranks of cadets, marching to the top.

There were only tulips. It just didn't seem proper to stop and talk to them, since he had his mind set on roses. He ambled through the trees until the path brought him to a small lake. He strolled to the end of a pier that jutted out into the calm blue water. As he sat down on a weather–beaten bench, a duck glided smoothly toward him. He wanted to shout at the duck, "Why?" The duck eased to a stop and stared at him. He quacked once, as if in answer, and Tom's brain spewed forth that horrible word, "cancer." Flooding his heart and brain were the emotions again. Why should she die in the prime of life? Because it was God's will. An answer, yes, but an inadequate one.

How long will these periods of grief and self–pity go on, he thought, reflecting on the past four months. Damn! It isn't right. How can a brain trample through so many varied thoughts almost simultaneously? Maybe I'm going crazy. No you're going through a normal process of grieving. The duck skittered along the surface of the water in his clumsy but effective way of becoming airborne.

That's the answer. Tom had to fly away to a new place. I have to leave the old life and not dwell on death. Death happens. It's normal. Must there be a reason? Maybe not.

Go. Get on with your new life.

Tom walked back toward the train station, somehow uplifted. There was a trace of spring in his steps. As he passed the field of tulips, he picked a large yellow one and cupped it in his hand. He looked down at the beautiful flower, smiled and thought, *life goes on and can be beautiful once again.*

CHAPTER TWO

The Lake Shore Limited was slowly pulling into Cleveland's AMTRAK station on time. The crowd of travelers lined the platform while waiting to depart.

Lea, dressed in a gray suit and a pink blouse, walked toward the train with her son, James. It was early spring and she could see the flowers beginning to bloom in the park across the street. The trees were bursting with green leaves. It was a good feeling to get away from Tom, her husband, and be free to make her decision.

James, a tall young man clad in blue jeans and white sweatshirt, stood next to his mother waiting patiently for the train to stop. He gazed at her with troubled eyes, realizing she was taking a giant step toward the rest of her life. "You're doing the right thing Mom. Come home with the right decision and no matter what it is, I'll understand. I love you."

Tears flowed from her eyes as she looked up at James and whispered, "It'll be what ever God wants me to do. He'll help me through this crisis." They hugged and kissed goodbye.

Lea boarded the train, looked sorrowfully back at James, and waved goodbye to him. She walked down the aisle looking for a seat next to a window. Plopping down heavily she adjusted her hand bag next to her feet and anxiously looked around at the strange faces. Leaning her head back against the seat, Lea closed her eyes and let out a deep sigh. Why am I here on this train?

Am I simply running away? Forty years of marriage is a long time. The memories of happiness and sorrow raced through her head in a rush of jumbled remembrances.

Her thoughts were interrupted by the conductor's voice on the intercom. "The train will be delayed for about two hours because of engine trouble. Sorry folks. Just sit tight and we'll get going as soon as possible," he announced. Lea let out another sigh. The moving scenery would have kept her mind occupied, but it couldn't keep her thoughts from turning to the past.

The two of us were high school sweethearts, the perfect couple. We were so much in love and needed each other. Our dreams and goals were going to set the world on fire. She let out a sad chuckle. She couldn't believe that she was contemplating a divorce. She rose and walked through the coaches. Entering the dining car she saw that it was warm and inviting. The tables were covered in red and white checkered tablecloths and each table had a small vase of fresh flowers. As she slipped into an empty booth, she caught the waiter's eye and ordered a cup of coffee. While sipping her coffee, a gentleman with a kind smile and strong, deep voice said, "Hello. Do you mind if I join you?"

His smile and small dimple on his right cheek was enticing to her. "If you like," Lea smiled timidly.

"Thank you," he said and ordered black coffee from the hovering waiter. An awkward quiet followed, prompting him to press on. "My name is Tom. Where are you going?"

"I'm traveling to Oregon to visit my sister. My name is Elizabeth. Call me Lea." She blushed.

"A lovely, musical sounding name. Lea, a beautiful nickname for Elizabeth." And his thoughts turned to the past.

Tom felt the need to confide in someone. "My wife died four months ago of cancer. I decided to take an eight thousand mile trip around the country. You might call it a therapy trip." He lowered his eyes, shifted uneasily in his chair, and looked up.

"I'm sorry to hear of your loss," Lea said. "I'm on a bit of a therapy trip myself. I'm taking time off so that I can make some decisions about my marriage to Thomas." He smiled at her. She smiled back. For some reason she felt relaxed and at ease with this man. Their conversation switched to happier topics and both found themselves laughing and agreeing on many things. They seemed like old friends, long lost, and now found, acting as if they hadn't seen each other for years. They talked of their children and happy events in their lives.

"Lea, may I join you for the rest of the trip to Chicago?"

"Fortunately no one is sitting in the seat next to me. It would be nice to have someone to talk to," Lea replied.

Lea was surprised at herself. She was easily confiding in a stranger.

As they settled in, Tom smiled and continued to talk about himself. "I'm a retired Air Force Lt. Colonel. I've traveled all over the world in my twenty–six years with the Air Force. I was in air defense radar duty." He paused. "Would you like to see some pictures of my family?"

Lea consoled him by sharing his pride and joy.

"This was my wife, Elizabeth, but we called her Nickie," "Hey, that's pretty odd, isn't it? She has your name and I have your husband's."

"Yeah, that's pretty strange and ironic," Lea agreed.

Tom paused, looked penetratingly at Lea, and thought of the names, the coincidence. Did it have a special meaning? Quickly looking back to the picture, he named his four children. "But enough about me. Tell me something about yourself. I'm really interested in your so called therapy trip. What happened?"

Lea hesitated, uncomfortable speaking about herself. But he seemed genuinely interested. She was at ease with this man, and knew she could pour her heart out to him. She glanced briefly out the window, then turned to Tom and started to quietly tell her story, feeling a great release of pent up emotions.

"The first twenty years of my marriage were happy years," Lea said nervously. "Three beautiful children were the joy of my life. Fishing trips to Canada were our vacations. But my husband couldn't keep a job for very long. He couldn't accept authority and changed jobs frequently. After the children were grown up and left home, my husband's philosophy of life became eat, work, sleep. There was no caring or looking to the future. I talked of leaving and divorce twice before. My husband's response was to threaten suicide. It amounted to blackmail to keep me with him. It worked twice, but not any more."

Engrossed in each other's stories, they didn't notice the miles that had slipped past. The train slowed entering Chicago. They were changing to different trains, here. Tom to Wisconsin and Lea to Oregon.

Tom was engulfed in his thoughts. He glanced at her as she sat there beside him. That glance brought him to the present time and place. Something about this petite little woman, her vulnerability, her distress, reached into his heart. It was not just pity. There was an attraction that was physical too. Her light auburn hair, her sparkling but sad eyes, her proud dignity even during troubled times, made Tom admire her. His thoughts turned to the realization that he was a lonely man. Could it be?

The train jolted to a stop.

They disembarked to the platform. Tom wrapped his arm around Lea's waist and they walked to the waiting room in the train station. It seemed so natural and so right. Their separate trains were leaving in a few minutes and it was time to part. Tom gave Lea his phone number in Florida, but didn't have the presence of mind to ask for Lea's number. They had to hurry. Tom put his arm around her, drew her to him, and kissed her lightly. Was this real? Was she this vulnerable, really this pliable? He felt an elation and an overwhelming sense of sexual desire. Lea did not resist. She looked up at him. He smiled and left hurriedly to catch his train.

Lea walked over to the desk to verify her connection. The clerk said, "Didn't your husband know which train to take?" Dumbfounded, Lea remarked, "He's not my husband."

"Oh!", blushed the clerk. "What is your destination?"

"Oregon," Lea replied.

"Sorry, there's been a mix–up. There won't be a train until nine tomorrow morning. Check in at the main office and they'll assign you a hotel room for the night."

Lea was devastated. In a strange town all alone, fear took over immediately. Through her forty years of marriage, she had never traveled alone. As she walked to the office she overheard a frantic mother with two young children talking to the ticket agent about missing the connection. He told her she would be taken care of, and not to worry. Lea went up to the woman cautiously and asked if they could share a room so she wouldn't be alone. She offered to help the lady with her children. The woman readily agreed and both women felt safer in the other's company.

CHAPTER THREE

Tom went on to visit friends and relatives across the country, spewing forth his grief and accepting their sympathy. It was good to get it out and not keep it bottled up inside. The trip held what he needed, diversions of all kinds to help him forget and to help him start forming a new life.

In Colorado Springs, visiting his mother and sister and her husband, he marveled at his sister's accomplishments as an artist. She was a member of a cooperative that owned a gallery called the Arati. Tom visited the gallery to view the work of several artists and sculptors from the area.

Peggy was putting the final touches on her latest sculpture. It depicted a man and woman entwined suggestively in love. It was a beautiful piece that Tom examined for some time. He said, "It's the essence of love," while standing before it.

Peggy asked, "What did you call it?"

Tom, embarrassed, said, "Oh, I, ah, I was just thinking how it looks just like the essence of love."

"That's perfect," Peggy replied. "Thanks, you've just named my latest piece." Tom was overjoyed and agreed to purchase it when completed.

Lucille, Tom's sister, had painted many beautiful pictures in oils and watercolors. However, her best medium was in the bas relief form that she learned while in Japan, where it is known as fucho–ga.

Her first work in this medium was titled "The Trail Boss." The low–relief sculpture of a craggy, weather–lined face, painted to make him seem alive, set Tom's mind to visualizing his story. He noticed the deep lines in the face and the steely look in the eyes. He must have been a trail boss on an old cattle drive. He could see him on his strong horse, making his way across the mountains fighting off rustlers and weather. Immediately the name, Clint, came to him for this rugged Westerner. Tom thought, *It's a good story for me to write when I get home.*

The next day Lucille and Bob drove Tom to Denver to resume his trip on AMTRAK. For this leg of the odyssey Tom had reserved a room, not a cramped little compartment. The sleeping car attendant briefed him on the amenities of this first class mode of travel. Coffee and orange juice would be delivered to his room at a time of Tom's choosing in the morning.

After getting settled, he went to the club car. With scotch and water in hand he settled into a window seat to admire the rugged scenery. He felt at ease. Thoughts of Nickie were less frequent. *Time is a heeling factor,* he thought. And he thought of Lea.

The train plunged into the foothills of the mountains, climbing through a pass ever higher. Old trails and roads nearly obliterated by new trees and brush could be seen on the hillsides. He slept that night peacefully, with no thoughts of the past.

When Andy, his attendant, brought orange juice and coffee in the morning he told Tom, "At about ten o'clock we'll be passing over a bridge above a river. Look down to the river on the left side of the train. You'll probably see river rafters there and they'll surprise you. I'll not tell you more. The surprise will either shock you or give you a chuckle."

"Okay Andy. Thanks."

At ten o'clock Tom was in the club car looking left out the window. As they rounded a curve he could see the bridge ahead. On the bridge he looked down, saw the rafters, and was shocked and amused. Two of the rafters, six–hundred feet below, were mooning the train. The other rafters were waving wildly.

The train arrived in Portland, Oregon so late that Tom missed his bus connection to Corvallis. He went to a phone in the station, looked up the number of an aircraft charter company at the local airport, and arranged a light aircraft flight to Corvallis. A Cessna and pilot were ready to fly. A taxi took him to the airport where he called his daughter, Marilyn.

John Barry, the pilot, and Tom took off for the ninety–mile flight. An overcast sky above their five thousand feet altitude cast a gloomy aura on the land below.

They arrived at their destination just before dusk, John flipped the switch to lower the landing gear. A red light glowed and the gear did not come down. He hit the switch again.

"Something's wrong. We'll have to make a wheels–up landing. Don't worry, we'll make it," John said.

Oh God, Tom thought, *not again,* as he remembered a similar emergency in 1957.

"Tower this is Cessna 157," John said into his microphone, "My gear won't come down. I'll orbit your field for fifteen minutes to burn off fuel, then belly it in. Over."

"Cessna 157 I copy. Recommend you land beside runway two seven zero, on the North side. We've had heavy rain and the ground is wet and soggy there."

"Roger tower, I'll call on final approach."

"Roger 157. Be advised no other aircraft are in the area."

"Tom, on final approach tighten your seat belt, lean forward and put your arms in front of your head. That soft wet ground is a big plus. We'll make it okay," John instructed.

Fifteen minutes later, John dragged the aircraft in low and slow just maintaining flying speed. The tail hit the ground first then the aircraft plopped down in the mud, skidding bumpily through the grass.

"When we stop get out quickly," John said.

"I know. Possibility of fire."

Tom opened the door as they slid to a stop and exited, with John following. There was no fire. As they waited nearby Tom thought, *how many charmed lives do I have?* Maybe I'll fly home from here and cancel the rest of the train trip. No you dummy. Quit being so pessimistic. Get on with your new life.

CHAPTER FOUR

Back in Florida after twenty–eight days of travel, Tom settled into the strange solitary life. After forty–two years of marriage to his beautiful Nickie, it was difficult. Meandering around his large four–bedroom house was unsettling, and cooking for himself was a tedious chore. Two of his children and their families lived nearby, though, and his three grandsons were a constant joy to him. At least he had that.

The days had warmed now, enough to heat the water in the swimming pool. Swimming every day was a therapy. Working around the house, mowing the lawn and trimming the bushes, ended in a cooling, relaxing dip in the pool.

One day as he relaxed on the chaise, he gazed at his back yard. It was beautiful. There, in one corner, was a tall, symmetrical Norfolk Island pine. The other corner was shrouded by a live oak, its huge spreading arms shielding half the lawn from the hot afternoon sun. In between was a gaudy, red flowered hibiscus, a shiny leafed schefflera, and a drab, but shapely when trimmed, olive bush. In the center of everything was a floppy, big–leafed shell ginger.

He relaxed on the chaise–lounge in the shade of the porch, gazing with pride at what he and Nickie had made of their home. It was good. Life was good, even though she was gone. He looked around again, proud of his well kept yard.

He saw a strange interloper in the middle of the shell ginger. *What's this spoiling my landscaping,* he thought. He hurried out to see the meddlesome intruder of dark green foliage. The tiny leaves on spindly branches looked weak and flimsy. This aberration, this weed, must go. He cut it down.

Two weeks later it was there again, but this time it had multiplied. Two offensive stalks had sprouted from the previously cut stump of weed. With ferocious perseverance, he cut it down again. No ugly monstrosity was going to spoil his lovely back yard.

Again, the weed's perseverance put his to shame. Three stalks shot up from the stump like Jack's beanstalk.

Tom decided to let it grow to see what happened. It thrived and grew fast. Soon the stalks were two or three inches thick and the pesky weed was fifteen feet high with fully leafed branches. It was definitely a tree. He called it the weed tree. He found Nickie's gardening book and looked to see what the monster was. Surely it was more than just a weed. Finally, he found it. The leaf form, the bark, the branch configuration—it all matched. It was called the albizia lebbeck tree.

So, he kept it, nurtured it, and began to think of it as enhancing the beauty of the back yard instead of hurting it. It's three sturdy trunks held fully leafed branches that shaded more of the lawn. Gazing reflectively at the albizia tree, the thought came forcefully into Tom's mind. *No matter what adversity, the albizia and I can weather it and come back even stronger.*

CHAPTER FIVE

Lea returned to Cleveland sooner than she had intended. Her decision to follow through with the divorce was final.

Life was too precious to spend her final days in misery. She would inform her husband as soon as she discussed it with Karen, their boss. She and Tom were apartment managers. The job required both of them for the management of the apartments and Lea wanted to tell Karen the news herself.

Monday morning Lea called for an appointment. Karen, a robust brunette, invited Lea into her office with a warm smile on her face.

"Hi Lea. Come in. Would you like a cup of coffee?"

"No, thank you," Lea replied nervously as she sat down.

Karen sensed something was wrong and closed the door to her office.

In a quivering voice Lea said, "Karen, what would happen to Tom's job if I decided to leave him?"

Karen, not blinking an eye, and not too surprised said, "He could maintain his position. He's a dependable, hard worker and we need him."

Lea was relieved. She had imagined Tom being thrown out of the apartment and unemployed, and was afraid he'd blame her for his loss. This would have made her feel guilty.

Karen said, "I'm not surprised about you and Tom. I've, noticed your unhappiness for a long time. As a matter of fact, I can't understand how you tolerated him this long. You deserve a medal. He's such a bore."

Lea's voice crackled. "Thank you. Karen, I'll hand in my resignation next Friday, allowing a two week notice. Is it possible to get a letter of recommendation?" Lea hesitated, looked down at her hands, then quickly back up at Karen. "Karen, I'm surprised. I never dreamed you'd be so understanding." Tears rolled down her pale cheeks and her voice quivered. "I just can't stand his self–pity anymore and…" She sobbed uncontrollably telling Karen of his threats of suicide.

"The last time he got out a gun and waved it around. With a wild, desperate look in his eyes he put it against his temple. He yelled, 'I swear, Lea, I swear I'll do it. I swear.'"

Lea shook her head to displace the terrible memory and the swell of disgust in her stomach. "I finally figured it out. His threats of suicide were blackmail—trying to keep me with him."

Karen rose and walked toward Lea who appeared so helpless. She comforted her, promised a letter of recommendation, and reassured her that she was doing the right thing.

Lea left the office and went back to her apartment to prepare for the biggest ordeal in her life. How was she going to break the news to Tom? She was afraid he'd become violent and threaten suicide. Lea was devastated. Her mind was whirling. Where would she go? What would she do for a job? There were so many problems and she was starting to panic. The decision had been made, and she was not prepared.

After dinner Lea approached Tom. He was sitting on the couch watching the news. "Tom, I'd like to discuss something very important with you. Can you bypass the news tonight?" The serious tone of her voice seemed to startle him.

"What's so urgent that I can't watch the news?" he said in an abrupt way.

Lea looked at him. Her hands were perspiring as she turned off the television. "Tom, I've made a decision about our life together. I've decided that I want a divorce."

Tom's mouth dropped open. "You want what? We have no problems. Your friends must be putting crazy ideas into your head."

"No they aren't. You know I've left you three times and came back three times because of your suicide threats. I know now that it's blackmail, and I'm not going to let you do it to me any longer. Our counseling has never worked because you don't want to change or even try to meet me halfway. It's always me who has to bend, and I'm tired of being a puppet on a string. I'm tired of being miserable."

Tom's face turned bright red as he stormed out to the kitchen and pulled open a drawer grasping a butcher knife. Lea sat frozen to her chair as he came back into the room.

He screamed at her, "Well, is this the way it must end? I'll never let you leave me."

"No," she shrieked. "Please, Tom, don't be like this. Calm down." Lea took a deep breath to get control of herself. Quietly she said, "Let's be mature adults and discuss our problem."

Tom, looking confused, let the anger edge out of his face. He threw the knife on a table near the couch and sat down in the rocker across from Lea. He started to cry uncontrollably. It was pathetic to see him so torn and defeated. It made Lea's heart ache.

She rose and left the room. There was no use trying to talk to him at this time, or any time. He needed counseling and it was up to him to seek it. She was exhausted trying to save their marriage, and needed to take charge of herself and do what was best for her.

Afraid he would attack her during the night, she retired to the spare bedroom and locked the door. Her mind was racing. She needed a plan to prevent a scene. Lea spent the night thinking. By morning she had a plan of action.

In the morning Tom left early to get his work orders at the office. Lea called Diana, their daughter.

"This is the Country Animal Clinic," said a voice on the phone. "How may I help you?"

"Is Diana there? This is her mother. It's urgent," Lea replied.

"Please hold." Lea tapped her fingers nervously on the counter top listening to the dull, tiresome music.

"What's so urgent, Mom?" Diana broke in, startling her mother.

Lea quietly answered, "Di, I have to leave your father. I can't handle it any longer. I'm afraid to be alone with him. Last night I told him I was leaving and he threatened me with a butcher knife." Lea stayed as calm as she could, but couldn't keep the anxiety out of her voice.

Diana said, "Oh God, Mom. How awful for you. You know I'm here for you. Just let me know when and how. Are you okay?"

Lea answered, feeling better by Di's concern, "Yes, I'm okay."

"Call me tonight when you know what's going on."

"Alright. Thanks Di. Love ya," she whispered and hung up the phone.

Lea felt relieved. Her plan was to leave on Friday night after Tom left for the men's bowling league. She'd give him the excuse of a throbbing headache. He won't have my cheering support this time.

Diana would come over with her van at seven and help her take everything needed for personal use to Diana's home. It's not the proper way to leave, she thought, but with his temper, it was the safest. That evening Lea called Diana to tell her the plan. She agreed it was a good one.

The week seemed endless until Friday, but it finally arrived. Tom left for bowling at six–fifteen. The weather was cold and a light snow was beginning to fall. Lea looked out the living room window at the gray November sky. Maybe she'd leave Cleveland to get far away from him.

Di was on time, thank goodness. She had a long way to come from Valley City, west of where Lea lived in The Towers. It will be wonderful to leave this apartment complex, Lea thought. She was responsible for cleaning vacant apartments, stairwells, elevators, hallways, and laundry rooms of nine floors. I'm sick of this type of work she thought to herself.

"Hi Di. I'm so glad you're on time," Lea said as she gave her a hug. "I can't wait to get out of here. I hope none of the tenants see us and start asking questions."

Diana responded with a warm hug and said, "Let's get the show on the road. Don't forget your golf clubs and bowling ball." It took two hours to load the van.

Lea felt a wave of relief pass through her as Di drove out of the parking lot. "I feel like a heavy load has been lifted off my shoulders. Thank you."

As she looked back at the apartment building, memories flashed across her mind of the good times and the bad. She wondered why their marriage had to end this way. Their dreams of setting the world on fire had ended long ago. A tear slowly rolled down her cheek as she turned around again and looked forward toward her future and a new life.

CHAPTER SIX

Even though some of his time was occupied in involvement with community affairs, Tom felt a huge void in his life. There was too much time to think of the past, and too much time speculating on the future. Lea came into his mind frequently. He couldn't stop thinking about her soft lips and sweet, smiling eyes. He yearned to see her, to kiss those pliable lips. Would she call? He felt stupid not getting her phone number.

And when he thought of Lea, he thought of Nickie in her last days. He couldn't get the haunting visions of her sick body out of his head. Did I do all possible to help her? Did I show her my love? He was tormented with remorse and guilt even though he knew he had done his best for her.

"Nickie, I loved you," he told her cold gravestone on his frequent trips to the cemetery. "I still love you. You were the best wife, the best mother. I miss you." It wasn't satisfying, but it helped him get through the grieving.

Sleepless nights were frequent. Work around the house or an occasional visit by the children and grand children interspersed his somewhat solitary life. He taught contract bridge once a week. It was invigorating. He was a director on his Homeowners Association Board, and a member of the county Board of Adjustment. But these jobs required his attention only once a month.

He had to fill the void. He couldn't go on immersed in thoughts of the past.

The next day he signed up for a creative writing class at the local Community College. A good time filler, he thought. And besides he had always wanted to try writing small short stories and his memoirs.

On the first day of class his instructor, Florence, asked, "Why do you want to write?"

Tom pensively replied, "I want to write about my life just as my mother did. My memoirs."

Florence countered, "But why? Why write them? What specific reason?"

"So my children and grand children will know. And, I'd like to try my hand at writing short stories."

"Great. And remember, your memoirs don't have to be chronological. That can be boring, like a textbook. First write something about your family and where you grew up."

Tom spent hours of struggling and searching for the right word or phrase, caught up in his many experiences and memories. He filled the next two months with furious writing. He learned some of the intricacies of the craft and thought about nothing else.

One of the diversions that enhanced his life was an occasional trip the Officer's Club at Patrick Air Force Base. There, the friendly bartender, Samantha (Sam) listened to his story.

"Your vest is covered with badges, wings and medals. Looks like you have them all," he said.

"Not really," Sam replied. "There always seems to be one more I haven't got yet from officers that come in here."

Tom studied the numerous decorations on her vest. "I don't see a flight nurse wings there."

"Flight nurse? I didn't know there was such a medal."

"I have it at home. I'll bring it to you the next time I'm up this way."

On the leisurely drive home, he reached back into the mists of memory and found his flight nurse, Joanna. Memories of her came in a nostalgic wave. He hadn't thought of lovely Joanna and the bomb in years. Vividly he saw Southampton, London, the Kensington Gardens Mansion, Hyde Park and the bomb. There in those scenes was Joanna. He leaned back with a wistful smile and relived those anxious yet beautiful days. They met on the Queen Mary, a huge passenger liner converted to a troopship. It was February 1944. As a young lieutenant he cautiously approached Joanna. "Hi," he said. His shy smile belied the bravado in his voice. "I 'm Tom. Would you like a coke?"

Joanna glanced at him a moment before she replied. "Well, sure," she replied confidently.

Her dimpled smile and pert way of tilting her head intrigued him. He went to the bar and came back with the soft drink. He joined her on the sofa in the plush lounge of the Queen of the seas. War was raging on three continents and life everywhere was focused on the war. For Tom and Joanna, war had taken over their lives. They lived with stress constantly and like everyone else, they talked about it.

"I'm a fighter aircraft controller," Tom explained, going into some detail but distracted by her disturbing nearness. Joanna told him she would be working in a field hospital near an airfield.

While she spoke, he marveled at her auburn hair, highlighted by the sun reflecting its rays through the port hole. He restrained himself from touching her ivory smooth skin. They seemed to find immediate rapport with one another, a sense of urgency flowing between them. Love happened quickly in those days, people making the most of time. There was never a promise of tomorrow.

They parted reluctantly at the end of the voyage to Southampton, England. She promised to meet him in London three weeks later. A soft gentle kiss, a last touching of fingers, and then she was gone.

He was impatient waiting for her at the Grosvenor House three weeks later. He watched her walk through the double doors, and marveled at her beauty, her slim long legs. She was as tall as he. Even in uniform, her firm breasts and seductively swaying hips excited him as no other woman had. At a nearby pub where they were ignored among the crowds of other service men and women, they quickly became intimate in their conversation. They held hands and more than once Tom found himself kissing those delicate fingers that he was sure wove magic on wounded patients. Their need for love and the protection of one within the other could not be denied. When they danced, he held her tightly, gently kissing her neck. He stroked her glistening hair. Her green eyes held a promise that gave him courage.

They walked to Hyde Park, hand in hand, in unspoken harmony. It was natural and compelling that they take a room at the quaint, old hotel across the street. The Kensington Gardens Mansion was grandeur from a long past era. Everything seemed oversize—the bed, the bureau, the wardrobe, the chairs. The windows overlooking the park were nearly as high as the ceiling. Curtains and draperies of dark blue tapestry hung gracefully at the sides of the windows. They clutched each other and kissed hungrily, collapsing into the plush chair. His hands roamed easily and unhindered. She kissed him passionately, powerful and turbulent emotions coursing through her. "Oh Tom." As he started to unbutton her blouse, she whispered "Come," and struggled up from the chair, unzipping her skirt. Tom fumbled expectantly with his shirt.

They quickly undressed, and even in their urgency donned night gown and pajamas. Joanna threw back the bed covers and gracefully slid into bed. Tom's emotions raced at the thought of the ecstasy to come. As he approached her, the incongruous wail of air raid sirens sounded. Tom stopped. Joanna sat up. They stared at each other. Joanna hurriedly left the bed and they went to the windows. Searchlights probed the sky while the drone of German aircraft engines sounded high above. They looked and listened in wonder at this frightening evidence of war. The crump of bombs striking their targets seemed far away.

The bomb whistled down mercilessly, perilously close, the conflagration of hell nearby. Tom quickly drew the draperies to protect them from flying glass. The missile exploded in Hyde Park across from the hotel. Fire raged, brandishing flames in all directions. The windows rattled, but didn't shatter.

The romance of only moments ago was snubbed out like the fire in the park as it was doused with water. Joanna looked wan and frightened, and trembled almost uncontrollably. The evening that promised romance, and perhaps the beginning of a deeper relationship, was ended. They were nearly strangers again, looking strained and even embarrassed. Whatever had been there was gone with the fragments of the bomb. They silently left the hotel. In haste, without goodbyes, with just a casual wave of the hand, they parted.

Tom's reverie ended. He became more aware of the road and the houses he was passing. The shroud of misty past changed to the clear glare of the present.

CHAPTER SEVEN

It was one of those times, the worst, because his brain was racing from one thing to another—incongruous thoughts, a jumble of ideas and subjects. Why was the weed tree dropping leaves, seed pods and blossoms. Should he start the story with dialogue, or use a descriptive scene to set the stage. Don't forget the hook. He watched a silly lizard climbing the screen, puffing up his throat sack, looking for food or his mate. It was also one of the best times because Tom was, at least to some degree, being creative—thinking of how to start the next story. As Tom sat down at his desk the phone rang.

"Tom Kelley here."

"Colonel Kelley? This is Lea, in Cleveland."

"Oh my God. Lea. You finally called. I've been waiting, wanting to hear your voice for these many months. I was such a fool not getting your number there in Chicago. How are you?"

"I'm okay. I've wanted to call for quite some time, but I was apprehensive about it. My children urged me to call. A lot has changed for me. Oh Tom, it's so good to hear your voice. Already I feel better."

"Did you reach a decision in Oregon? What are you going to do?"

"I've decided to get a divorce. It's the only solution for me. And my children all say, do what you think is right."

"Well, they're right," Tom answered. "You need to do what will make you happy."

"I agree. I'm sorry but I have to make this a short call. Please write to me at my daughter's address."

They exchanged addresses.

Tom excitedly said, "I'll sit down tonight and write a letter. I'm so happy you called."

Elizabeth hurriedly replied, "I have to go. I'll write and tell you what's happened. Bye, Tom."

"Bye, Lea, and best wishes."

Tom was ecstatic. He jumped up from the telephone, went out to the porch and looked up at the full moon. Wonderful. Thank you, God. He went immediately to his writing table to start the letter.

During the next two months, a steady flow of letters and phone calls poured across the miles. Tom flooded the mail route between Florida and Ohio like a downpour of rain inundating the land. He became more bold in his letters as time passed. From statements of 'wish you were here,' and 'I'd like to take you to my favorite restaurant,' to the brazen suggestion that Lea fly down for three or four days.

In his next phone call he ventured, "We need to talk and get to know each other better. After all, five hours on the Lake Shore Limited was a mere introduction. And I have to find out if I was dreaming or not when I felt those softest lips. For me, it was like the feathery touch of a wispy cloud kissing a mountain peak. How did I have the nerve to kiss you after knowing you for only five hours? You were so small, vulnerable and beautiful. It seemed natural and right."

"Yes, for me it was also the natural thing to do."

Lea's letters were more reserved but as time went by she poured out her heart. She told him of the horrible scene with her husband when she told him she wanted a divorce. And she told of vacating their apartment and moving to her daughter's house. The trauma of her divorce was evident in her writing. But she was coping and writing her thoughts.

"Tom, it was your letters, read over and over again, that gave me the courage to follow through on my convictions. I'm responsible for my own happiness. The seminar and retreat counseling have opened my eyes too. I have to try to find happiness in a new life. How could I continue to live with a man whose only philosophy of life was *work, eat, sleep?*"

Although she had never been to Florida, Lea pictured sandy beaches and warm sun. She had lived in California for five years, and she wrote to Tom of her love of swimming. "I've been swimming near San Diego and in Hawaii. I hope some day we can walk your beaches. I can picture the sand, the surf, the sun."

When Tom read that letter, he focused on the words "picture the sand." Of course. He had told her a few letters ago that he would send a copy of one of his stories. It was only natural to send "A Picture in the Sand," one of his experiences while in the Air Force.

Lea eagerly opened Tom's package. It was a heavy, thick one. She had guessed correctly. It contained one of his stories.

A PICTURE IN THE SAND

"When we touch down, put on your helmet. Remember, we've got ten minutes at the outside, no more. The clock starts ticking the second the wheels hit the beach," Lt. Flynn, the pilot, said.

"Gotcha." Kelley nodded automatically. The pilot's warning was always the same. It might be phrased a bit differently, with a few colorful phrases thrown in, but it was routine. Pilots were briefed to warn the passenger, not question him and although pilots varied, the passenger was always Major Tom Kelley.

Kelley took a nervous breath. More than anyone else, he realized the critical timing of these short flights that were dependent on the moon, the tides, and the North Koreans. Such flights were always a prelude to longer ones, wrapped in a cocoon of secrecy. While he seemed calm and reassuringly casual, in his heart was a tiny, gnawing apprehension. *What if my luck runs out* he wondered? He dismissed the thought from his mind, forcing himself to smile in a show of bravado.

At the end of the runway on their base in Osan, Korea, Tom shouted over the engine noise, "Let's go!"

Lt. Flynn advanced the throttle and the small, light aircraft leaped into the air, bound for the island of Pyongyang–Do. Americans called it "P–Y–DO." It was an island off the South Korean coast. Its unique location placed it treacherously close to North Korea, too.

At night the long tentacles of North Korean searchlights stretched to the island. The landing beach was well within range of enemy artillery. The big lights began their vigil as soon as the last sliver of sun slipped into the abyss of shadows beyond the horizon. There was a ten minute window of time when they could escape detection.

Even though it was 1958 and the shooting in the Korean police action had ended, tensions were high. No one trusted the North Koreans.

The last splash of outrageous color invaded the small aircraft as Tom gazed at the sunset. He was fascinated, watching in awe as the dancing swirls of copper and gold blended into the wild patterns of a kaleidoscope. Nature was the ultimate artist. Those colors were her strokes on the palette of the sky. From somewhere beyond, faint tinges of pink and purple heralded the approach of twilight. Soon, in symbiotic genuflection, the colors would kneel to the inevitable blue sapphire of night.

He wondered if he could put his feelings into words and do justice to the panorama of sunset, sky, and sea. He looked at his watch. There was little time to be a poet. Already the sun was almost below the horizon, but there it was—the fleeting glimpse of green topping the sun in breathtaking beauty.

Kelley blinked to shut out the invading rays. He had a job to do. He was a cog in a loop of secrecy that demanded his careful attention and concentration. Once they were on the beach, he had ten minutes before his life and the pilot's were endangered.

He had gotten into this maelstrom of intrigue because of his position as Chief Controller at the Division Control Center. He and only two other officers knew of this secret, highly dangerous military operation. Lives and an entire government might depend on him doing his job. The uniform became his master, and the poet was stifled.

After thirty minutes of low flying, they approached the island where one of their radar sites was located. At low tide, the hard–packed sand became their landing strip. Even as they touched down and rolled lightly down the beach, a radar officer emerged from the shadows to meet the plane. Kelley jumped down and motioned the man to follow him a few yards past the aircraft. The pilot turned around, ready to take off again.

Kelley knelt on the beach and outlined a picture in the sand with his finger. It was a crude drawing of the island and the coastlines of North and South Korea. He drew a line from southeast to northwest, bisecting the island.

"Tonight at twenty–three forty–five," Kelley said, "your radar may pick up an aircraft flying this track and near this point." He touched the map. "It'll be flying northwest at extremely high altitude." Kelley looked the man in the eyes. "It'll be a B–Fifty–seven Canberra."

The officer, a lieutenant, met Kelley's glance, then shrugged. "Sure. I got it." He nodded, but he sounded skeptical.

Kelley squared his shoulders. Even in the fading light he saw the question in the mans eyes. He cleared his throat to speak with more authority. "Should your men wonder about the altitude, remember, it's still a B–Fifty–seven Canberra."

They locked eyes for a second, then the officer stepped back and shrugged. "Right."

Kelley stepped forward. "You will not, repeat, not report this one to the Control Center. You kill the report right here. Understand?"

The radar officer hesitated. "As you say, it's not there."

"You got it," Tom said.

With a nod, Kelley mumbled a hasty parting word. The officer saluted him but Kelley didn't notice as he ran toward the airplane. The pilot had the plane rolling on the beach even as Kelley scrambled aboard. North Korean searchlights would be spreading deadly fingers of light in less than seventy seconds. They had barely enough time to get out of reach.

Kelley sighed with relief and settled back, momentarily closing his eyes as they became airborne.

At 2300 hours, Major Kelley strode briskly to the Osan Control Center. He was chief controller of the center into which all radar reports were funneled. If the P–Y–Do report on the U–2 aircraft somehow got through, he'd suppress it on the spot.

When midnight passed without any report coming in, he took a long breath. That time, P–Y–Do did its job, but it was getting more and more difficult to be convincing. The public didn't know about the U–2, and no other aircraft could fly as high. This was why the blip on the radar screens had to go unreported.

The next morning at the general's daily briefing, Kelley initiated his section of the report with the carefully chosen words, "P–Y–Do is operational." He paused and looked at the general and the colonel. They didn't speak, but each gave him a slight nod.

They knew what he meant, but they were the only ones present, other than Kelley, who did. The U–2 secret was safe.

Lea slowly put the story down in her lap, and leaned her head back. Wow, she thought, what a life this man has had in the Air Force. What an adventurous life. He 's probably got many more stories to tell. That night she dreamed of a handsome, blue eyed officer lying next to her telling exciting stories.

CHAPTER EIGHT

He didn't care. Even though he knew the chance of seeing her was doubtful, Tom called his travel agent.

"Book me on a flight to Cleveland, Bill. I want to arrive during the day of September fourteenth."

In about twenty minutes Bill called back with the flight information. "When do you want to return, Tom?"

"The seventeenth."

Bill punched it in on his computer and read the schedule to Tom.

"I'll be in tomorrow to get the tickets," Tom said. On the morning of September 14th, Tom left early for the airport. He didn't mind waiting. It was fun watching the people rushing or ambling to the gates. He would speculate on each one of them and wonder what their story was, their problem, their future.

He arrived in Cleveland on time. He got a room at a hotel near the airport and went to the lounge for a drink and information.

"Where does one go to have a good time and a good dinner?" he asked the friendly bartender. The bar was nearly deserted.

"You have two choices," the bartender replied. "First there is the "Flats" near downtown Cleveland. It's a rejuvenated area with lots of nightclubs and restaurants and shows. Or you can go over to the other side of the airport to the 100th Bomb Group restaurant. You can see it from here. Look behind you out the windows."

Tom didn't have to look out the window. His choice would be the 100th Bomb Group. After a one hour nap in his room, he picked up the phone to call Lea's daughter. They had recently agreed to use the name T.J. for Tom because her husband was a Tom and Lea preferred to call him T.J.

"Good afternoon, Diana. This is T.J. in Florida. Is Lea there?" He didn't want it known that he was in Cleveland.

"Oh, hi T.J.. Mom isn't here. She went to Michigan to visit friends there. She'll be back in about a week."

Dejected, Tom said, "Thanks Diana. I'll call later. Hope all is well there. Goodbye for now." No use getting into a long conversation. He had never met Diana anyway and now was not the time for small talk.

As he put the phone down a salient thought came to him. The old Air Force axiom—do something, don't just sit there. Do something even if it's wrong. Well, he did something and it was wrong. He didn't check to see of Lea would be there.

The restaurant exuded the atmosphere of World War II England and an 8th Air Force B–17 bomber headquarters. The building was styled like an English country house, not a manor house. The entrance was lined with sandbags and a heavy, old wooden door opened into a dimly lit passageway to the reservations desk. The maitre d'hotel directed him to the bar. A large dance floor surrounded by tables adjoined it. Through the large windows he could see the patio covered with a roof that had large holes in it as if it had been bombed. It was a realistic scene of the war years.

It was seven o'clock in the evening as Tom slid onto a bar stool at one end of the bar. Ordering a scotch and water he, as usual, asked the bartender's name. Maury was friendly and Tom introduced himself.

"Is that short for Maurice?" Tom asked.

"No, that's it." He spelled it.

"When does this place liven up?"

"By nine o'clock we'll be crowded and jumping," Maury said.

Tom had two drinks, then dinner, and back to the crowded bar. Maury placed Tom's B&B in front of him and asked, "How was your dinner?"

"The prime rib was excellent."

The patrons at the bar and on the dance floor were noisy and laughing. Their average age seemed to be about forty.

After finishing his drink, Tom left. He was tired and needed a solid sleep. He decided to come back the next night and see if he could fit in with the younger crowd.

After a lazy day of watching television, a little walking, resting, and thinking of Lea and her gentle kiss, he went to the 100th Bomb Group. After pausing to look at pictures and mementos in the hallways and rooms, reminders of WWII and B–17 bombers, he went into the bar. Maury was there.

"Scotch and water, Tom?"

"Yes. You're a good man, Maury, remembering my drink."

After an hour the bar was crowded and Tom was talking to his bar stool mates. They were friendly, fortyish men and women. Another hour passed and Tom overheard someone say, "Take care of the old codger down at the end of the bar." Taking no offense, Tom instead felt a sense of welcoming care.

"Get me an order of stuffed mushrooms, please," Tom said.

"Right away," Maury replied.

By eleven, everyone at the bar knew Tom's name. They offered to buy his drinks and asked where he was from and how come he was here.

Sherry, about forty–five years old, was sitting next to him. She was a petite brunette with a sensual figure who didn't mind showing it. Her low–cut pink blouse exposed the tops of her breasts. Around her neck was a thin gold chain on which hung a small white rose pendant, which rested in her cleavage. As he stared at the pendant and her bosom, Tom was reminded of his story, "The White Rose Pendant."

Sherry asked, "What brings you to Cleveland?"

Tom responded, "Well, it's a case of an old man trying to get started in a relationship with a lady. If you want more of this story I'll continue. Can I buy you a drink, Sherry?"

"I'll have another bourbon and ginger. Tell me more."

Tom ordered her drink and Maury brought him one on the house. He turned to Sherry, and told his story. The girl was very attentive.

"You're quite a guy," Sherry said. "And I think you're doing the right thing. Your trip gave you time to clear your thinking. And as for your second love, go for it."

Maury brought the stuffed mushrooms. Sherry fed them to Tom— her fingers to his mouth, really taking care of the old codger. After all, a seventy year old man needs all the help he can get.

Sherry said, "Come on. Let's dance."

Tom protested a little because the music was rock and roll. But then he thought, *why not give it a try*. He replied, "Okay, but you better put on your steel toe shoes. You'll have to teach me." He kept up with her quite well, faking it and trying to imitate her and the other dancers. Two numbers were enough and they retired to their bar stools. After finishing the stuffed mushrooms, which turned out to be his dinner, Tom informed his friends, "One more drink and I have to leave." After objections all around, Tom continued, "I have to get my beauty sleep you know."

"Beauty?" Sherry asked.

"You're right," he replied, "No beauty here. Truthfully, I have to rest the weary old bones."

Bob on the other side of him said, "We know you're an old codger, but you sure don't act like one."

Tom finished his last drink and turned to Sherry. "Your beautiful white rose pendant reminds me of a short story I've written. The title is 'The White Rose Pendant'. I think I'll rewrite it and make you the main character. I'll send you a copy when it's finished. Is that okay?"

"Wonderful. Just a minute while I write down my address."

While she wrote, Tom's mind again turned to Lea. Why did she go away? How I'd love to see her—her sparkling but sad eyes, her pert little figure. Stop it you old fool.

"Here you are Tom," Sherry said.

He took the little scrap of paper. "I'm leaving everyone. Good night."

CHAPTER NINE

Tom returned home frustrated and discouraged. He threw his suitcase on the bed, made himself a stiff scotch and water and stomped out to the back porch. After two big gulps he sauntered to the edge of the pool, stared at the albizia tree and blurted out, "You have it easy, tree. You don't have a brain that plods through a morass of troubled thoughts. There's no chaos in your existence." Wrong, he thought. Remember you created chaos and tumult in the albizia's life.

Damn it you old fud. Get out there in the crazy world and do something that can unwind your mind, ease the tension. Yeah, do something.

His thoughts immediately proceeded to women. Lea. I might never get to her. Nickie. Gone forever. Betty Williamson, the flight nurse, lost in the melee of war. Alicia Charbonneau. A teenage flirtation. Marisa. A good friend. Yes perhaps Marisa would do it. She'd unwind me. Marisa, with the musical sounding name, widow of a fellow officer Tom had been stationed with at Tyndall Air Force Base. She lives in Vero Beach. They exchanged Christmas cards. Maybe she'd go to dinner with him. I'll call her.

"Well Tom. Nice to hear from you. What's the occasion?" Marisa said.

"Nothing momentous. I wondered if you would like to go to dinner and talk about old times at Tyndall. Sometimes I miss the sound of jets and small talk in Air Force jargon. Remember those days at the officers' club?"

"Sure do. I don't miss the jets, but I do miss the good times at the club. I'd love to go to dinner."

Visions of various ecstasies traversed his mind as he drove to Vero. But would Marisa be of the same mind? I hope so, he thought. She sounded eager to see him. Tom recalled parties at the Club where friends exchanged partners on the dance floor. Marisa was a lovely lady, black hair, lithe and pliable while dancing. Her pert little nose was enhanced by full, sensuous lips. He remembered it was difficult to concentrate on dancing with her in his arms. You dreamer, you. Relax. Let's see what happens.

At the Red Tail Hawk they toasted to the good old days and enjoyed snapper almondine. The conversation was easy as they recalled events at the base. Even the sad time of Jack, Marisa's husband's death was spoken of with ease. It was a long time ago.

"Tom, I've always wondered if you were given orders to be the one to break the news to me that Jack had crashed?"

"Yes and no. I was given the order, but I had planned to do it anyway. After all, I was on the radio telephone with him when he declared an emergency. He flamed out at low altitude and couldn't eject. He went into the gulf with the aircraft."

"As you guys say, he bought the farm. I can say these things now. I can talk about it. It was so long ago. I figured you'd be the one to come to my house."

"Enough. Let's dance. This trio is playing our kind of music. There's 'Moonlight Serenade', a nice dreamy one."

He held her lightly as her body pressed against him. The fragrance of her hair, her soft but firm breasts excited the inner Tom. They danced eloquently together. Again he thought of the Club at Tyndall.

Tom raised his glass of brandy to Marisa's creme de menthe and said, "To us. May our pleasure with each other continue this evening."

She hesitated slightly and looked into his eyes. "If that says what I think you mean, perhaps we will continue. To us."

The drive to Marisa's house was eerily quiet. Each was immersed in their own speculation, their own cautioned eagerness. They both sensed that this was to be a fleeting tryst, a temporary rendezvous. They glanced at each other occasionally with a wry smile, and they knew what each other was thinking.

Arm in arm they strolled to the front door. Marisa handed Tom the key. He enfolded her in his arms and they kissed long and hungrily. She pushed away from him and guided his key hand to the door lock. Inside, she turned abruptly to him.

"Tom, somehow you've turned me into kneadable clay, easily shaped. But I don't care. I need you as much as you need me. Come with me."

She quickly flicked the bedspread from the bed and started to undress. Tom eagerly shed his clothes as he marveled at her beauty. She was a trim, well endowed woman, looking younger than her years.

Their sexual union was both gentle and furious. Slow loving erupted into a frenzied search for fulfillment. It was as if their time was limited, as if they knew it would be over too soon. But they extended their probe for, their search for loving consummation. They reached the pinnacle of their mountain of desire.

They slept entwined together.

CHAPTER TEN

Tom had left Marisa's house quietly before she awoke. He left a senti-
mental little note on the kitchen table expressing his feelings and gratitude. He knew she was aware of the urgency and true nature of their
rendezvous. A release, a moment of love, not to be forgotten, not to be
repeated. Tom had known it would be that way too. But his lady had to
be Lea. After three drafts of a letter, trying to get it just right, he started
typing.

> *Dear Lea,*
>
> *Let me attempt to explain some things. When we met on the
> train, we were both coping with our own problems. That was the
> foremost thing in our minds. I really enjoyed talking to you and
> appreciated your sincerity and candid revelations about your life.
> It helped me to take my mind off my own problem, and realize
> that other people needed understanding too.*
>
> *Let me quote from the preface to my story about my "Eight
> Thousand Mile Therapeutic Trip." "Nickie died recently. All
> knew her as a loving wife, a wonderful mother, and a great lady.
> She is gone, but life goes on—for me a new life. I decided that the
> thing I needed at the moment was a long trip around the USA."*
>
> *The pertinent phrase in the preface that concerns you and me
> is, "for me a new life". I have come to believe that you may be part*

of that new life. By this I don't mean a rigid commitment. But I really want to see you and talk about future "new lives."

Of all the people I spoke to on my trip, you were the one who stayed with me in my mind. The crowning glory and the cement that fixed you in my mind was your goodbye kiss in the Chicago train station. I was surprised and elated.

Now the mundane. Sunday will be my birthday, the big "70." But I feel about 50. Sometimes the minor aches say 60.

Hurry down here to help me enjoy the eighty–seven degree water in my swimming pool. Also, when you come, we will go to the Officers Club at Patrick Air Force Base. I'm a member there. We'll have a great time. I know that I'm being impatient. Can't help it. Wish you could find a way to take a trip to Florida, a short vacation to get away and think further about your situation.

Hope I get your letter or phone call tomorrow.

Love,
T.J.

It was time to teach bridge. The classes were conducted at the Yacht Club situated on the St. Lucie River. His reputation of being a good teacher who made his classes fun assured that there would be enough students. His class consisted of sixteen people, mostly women. At the beginning of the fifth class, he admonished his students.

"All right class, I'm going to check your knowledge of no trump. If you had studied just a little, you would know that fourteen points is not enough to open the bidding with one no trump. But that's okay. Try it and learn," Tom said. "If any of you make the three no trump bid, I'll buy your coffee."

They were playing on the porch at the Yacht Club overlooking the river. It was a beautiful day—warm, no wind, with white puffs of fleece slowly wending their way across the blue sky. Tom noticed that one of the clouds resembled a playing card. *Which one,* he thought? The flipping of cards behind him brought him back to the reality of the moment. They were struggling to make their no trump bids. He strolled over to the third table and examined Clair's cards. Of course she was an attractive, blonde haired lady. What a great job this is, he thought, as he looked at this stunning woman in her sky blue dress. He thought of Lea. She was stunning and beautiful. He forced himself back to the chore at hand, pointing to the card she should play.

He moved on to table two. The blue dress of table one prompted him to glance at the same colored sky. His card cloud was slowing down, disengaging itself from the other suds–like puffs of whitewash that painted the sky. It seemed too, that it was lower than the others. Edith, the elderly lady at table two, questioned him. "What should I bid?" A quick perusal of her cards dictated an opening bid of one spade. She dutifully but unsurely bid it.

"Please," Tom said. "Say it with conviction. You know it's right. If I'm wrong you get a cocktail of your choice, and I'll join you." The bidding proceeded to the expected final bid of game—four spades. The unimaginative lead of the two of clubs started the play.

Tom felt a need to look at the cloud again. Sure enough, as he expected, it was closer and lower, and had become a dark gray in color. The other clouds had scuttled away as if their darker playmate had contracted a horrible social disease. *I'll be damned,* Tom thought, *it has form. It's a knave. It's the jack of spades.* The shape was clear. Now it was larger and nearly black. Even the face on the card shaped cloud was becoming vivid. True to form, there was only one eye on the knave, and the hand held a misshapen figure eight. Was this a portent of some kind? He stiffened with tension.

Usually cool and unperturbed, Tom stared nervously at the cloud, completely forgetting the class. *I must have an overly colorful imagination,* he thought. But then he remembered the four spade bid and turned quickly to table two. Was there an omen concerning this bid, this hand? Edith held the jack of spades and the three of clubs, the last two cards in her hand. She looked up at Tom, obviously not knowing which card to lead.

Tom glanced quickly at the cloud, as if to ask its advice. It was mostly black with the knave a dirty white. The eye of the knave seemed to blink and the weirdly shaped eight in the hand suddenly became a bolt of lightning, arcing down into the river. The crack of thunder made everyone jump, and the matron's jack of spades fell to the table. The players recovered their composure and played their cards. The opponents' ten of spades fell, and Edith's lowly three of clubs, the thirteenth club, was good, making the game.

"Would you have played the jack of spades?" Tom asked.

Edith answered, "Truthfully, no."

"Fate and a knave of a cloud allowed you to make your bid."

"What?"

"Nothing. Maybe it was the thunder that made you play the right card, the knave of spades," Tom answered.

When he returned home from the bridge lesson, Tom sank into his chaise on the porch, looking at the clear blue water in the pool. The class was fun and unique. Ah, the knave of spades, the thunder, the matron, the intriguing blue dress which matched the color of the sky. And then he thought of the Lake Shore Limited, then Sam at the Officers Club, and the tryst and the bomb in London. He looked away from the pool, hoping the diverse thoughts would slow down. Lea came forward prominently. Her last letter was not encouraging.

CHAPTER ELEVEN

Dear Tom (T.J.),

Here I am at the retreat for healing the person within. We are supposed to write a letter to someone we need to let our innermost feelings out to, and you came to my mind.

I'm looking out over Lake Erie, sitting in a lawn chair under an old oak tree and trying to figure out why God has put you into my life. I feel you will understand my feelings without making fun of me or ignoring them. It's so peaceful here away from the sounds of the city. There's just the sound of birds chirping, a crow cackling, and the soft roll of a wave or two on the beach During this retreat, I'm learning that I've been hurting a lot and have been suppressing it. Your letters have been very uplifting. Your openness has made me realize there are men one can confide in and who can understand my feelings. It's a nice inner calmness to know you care.

On my journey to Oregon I met many men and women, but you stood out the most. As you said in your letter, you realized that other people have problems and it helped you to forget your own. So, people need people to survive and feel worthy. I'm having such mixed emotions about my marriage. Thirty–nine years is a long time with one person, and there are many ties, good and bad to consider. Oh, how confusing my thoughts and memories make me.

Rather than getting our hopes up for a possible new life together, we had better put a hold on it indefinitely. My husband wants to go to a marriage counselor, so it seems it's God's will for us to salvage our marriage. I really would like to pursue our friendship, but I'm too confused to decide what is best for me. I plan to cancel the Post Office box and let still waters lie still.

God Bless You,
Best Always,
Lea

Crestfallen, Tom let the letter fall to his lap, leaning his head back. His hopes were nearly shattered, but he was not one to give up easily. I'll get right at my trusty, ancient typewriter and try to calm her confused mind. I have to convince her that her decision to terminate her marriage was the right one.

His brain unexpectedly turned to a completely unrelated thought. Or was it unrelated? No! The image of a woman he had never met came upon the scene. Irena. Irena Charbonneau, mother of the girl who had fed him stuffed mushrooms at the 100th Bomb Group restaurant. Sherry had given him her mother's address in Jacksonville, Florida. She was the widow of a Navy officer. Sherry evidently thought he would be a good companion for her lonely mother.

No, he thought, it's Lea I want. Get busy on that letter. Tell her your inner–most thoughts. Tell her you need her.

He looked out across the pool at the albizia tree, the weed tree. It had come through the ravages of nearly being killed two times. And the tree had come back stronger than ever, with three sturdy trunks. It was now in full bloom, hardy, and showing the world it was here to stay. Persistence. The tree had it. Again, the phrase "do something" creased his mind, and this time, do something right. It was right to get and keep Lea.

CHAPTER TWELVE

It was mid afternoon. Time for a cocktail, his usual screwdriver, and a quick dip in the pool. Then a call to Diana's home to talk with Lea. The drink and the dip buoyed his spirits and he hoped for the best in the phone call.

"Lea, how are you? I just had to call after receiving your letter. I was worried that you wouldn't call or write again. The job sounds like a good move for you to make. And the training session in Columbus should be helpful."

"Yes. It seems good to me too. I'm really excited about it. Maybe this new job will help me get my head on straight again. I'm still confused on what to do. How are you?"

"I'm fine. Just got out of the pool. The water is eighty–four degrees and delightful. Wish you were here to enjoy it with me. Did you get my letter and tape that I mailed three days ago?"

"No, no letter or tape. The last letter was dated a week ago. Anything exciting you're sending me?"

"Oh, I don't know. The tape is big band music. I wanted you to hear one particular song on it. "September Song" is the title. After you listen to it, give me a call. I'd like to know your impression of it. Call me collect if you want."

"Okay, T.J.. I have to go now. Diana and I are going shopping. I'm looking forward to the letter and the tape. Bye."

"Goodbye, Lea. Take care and keep the faith."

The next day Tom decided to take a chance and went to see his travel agent. He arranged a flight to Columbus, Ohio that would get him there a day after Lea arrived. He would stay for five days.

Lea called the next day. She had received Tom's letter and tape. She seemed very happy and more animated than usual. She seemed to be bubbling over with enthusiasm and the sound of her voice made Tom think that perhaps a new era was about to dawn in their relationship.

"T J., your letter gave me renewed courage to continue my effort to build a new life. And I love that song, September Song. It applies to us. Two senior citizens, both with a chance at a second start, a second chance at happiness. Maybe we can find that chance soon with each other. I've decided to continue my procedure to get the divorce. My lawyer's working on it and it shouldn't be too long a wait. Again, you have boosted my spirits and I wish I could see you soon.

"Lea, I…"

"Wait T.J.. I have to say the next thing quickly before I lose my courage to say it. It's so uncharacteristic of me. Could you come up to Columbus while I'm there going to school? We have to see each other more and talk about the future."

"I'll be there with bells on. I was hopping I could come to see you soon and this seems to be the perfect time. I'll see my travel agent tomorrow and arrange a flight. I'll arrive the day after you get there. I'll let you know the flight number and arrival time. This is wonderful. Thank you for inviting me to come to Columbus. See you soon."

"Okay. It'll be wonderful seeing you. Bye for now."

Visions of a rendezvous in a motel there danced in Tom's head. But wait, he thought. *Perhaps I'm getting ahead of myself, and too far ahead of Lea.*

As arranged, Lea was there to meet him. He dropped his one suitcase and hugged Lea. She looked radiant, but she appeared tentative and nervous. He kissed her lightly on the cheek.

"Lea, it's so good to see you. You look wonderful. Thanks for taking the time to meet me. I know you're busy."

"I'm glad you're here, T.J. You'll calm my flustered mind and maybe I can concentrate on my studies. Come. My car is nearby."

It was a cold November afternoon. A gray somber sky ushered in a few lazily falling snow flakes. The warmth of the car and Lea's presence made Tom feel good. He realized that he was pushing her hard and quickly. But she was there and she was receptive to some degree.

Lea was essentially a home–body, never before taking an adventurous risk in her associations with men other than her husband. Tom had been writing to her of adventure—her adventure into the world of a new life, possibly with him.

One letter said: "I realize that my suggestion that you come to Florida is a somewhat bold one, but I think it's the right thing to do. Granted you have to solve the complicated situation there. I understand, too, your statement that you are the old fashioned girl type. That's okay. Mix that with a bit of adventurism soon and we can be happy." And then in another letter: "Lea, if you would come down to see me and stay a few days, we would get to know each other as we should. Of course, you could stay at my house, with no obligation to do anything you don't want to do. I'd like to see you happy for a change, after all the problems you've had. Please do all you can to make the trip and venture into a new life."

They arrived at the Shamrock Motel where Lea was staying. It was near where her schooling took place. Tom was elated that Lea had only one room. He hugged her tightly and kissed her passionately. Lea responded with passion, but Tom could feel her tentative, somewhat stiff reserve.

"I know that I'm coming on strong, but I can't help it. You just tell me to back off or slow down and I'll do it. Let's go and have dinner. A friend of mine recommended the Jai–Alai restaurant".

She said, "Be patient with me. I'm trying to adjust, trying to put some of the past forty years out of my mind. I'm finding out that divorce is a traumatic experience. You were right when you wrote that perhaps divorce is more difficult to accept than death. Mine was a matter of choice, whereas you had no choice when your wife died. But I can't dwell on this now. Let's go to your restaurant."

They drove into Columbus to the Jai–Alai. T.J. ordered his favorite dinner—veal Oscar while Lea chose a filet mignon. The conversation was mundane and pointedly skirted around Lea 'a turmoil of recent divorce proceedings and her meeting with T.J.. With a glass of chablis they clinked glasses as T.J. toasted, "a votre sante".

"What does that mean?" Lea asked.

"It's French. To your health. I picked up a few phrases during the war, and I had a year of French in high school."

Tom rated his veal Oscar. In his travels throughout the country he ordered his favorite entree frequently and rated it on a scale of one to ten. The Jai–Alai rated low—only a five. The veal was sliced too thick and was tough, and the bernaise sauce only mediocre. He told Lea that so far, the best veal he'd had was at a German restaurant in Milwaukee, Wisconsin. As they finished their after dinner drinks, B&B for Tom and Creme de Mint for Lea, they still talked of anything but her travails.

A light fluffy snow slowly penetrated the cold Ohio air. It stayed on the ground and seemed to purify the atmosphere. As Lea drove to the motel, Tom talked lightheartedly of the sunny warmth of Florida versus the cloudy cold of Ohio. "Yes, the snow's beautiful. But how nice is it when it's dirty in the streets, and it gets deep enough to shovel. In Florida, the heat and humidity are problems easily solved by my swimming pool and air conditioning." Gentle persuasion was the key. He knew that Lea thought he was a nice guy. Now, he had to help her overcome the mental strain of terminating a forty year marriage.

At the motel, a seemingly natural and unseen wall separated them in the king size bed. It was a wall of reticence and shyness on Lea's part, and measured restraint on Tom's part. They talked until sleep could not be denied. They rested fitfully until morning. A mostly silent breakfast at the Red Barn restaurant across the street, and then Lea hurried off to class.

The snow dropped at a forty–five degree angle hurried along by a cold North wind. The temperature was twenty degrees and the snow was starting to pile up. It was five inches deep. Tom couldn't hibernate in the warm motel room all day so he ventured out into the near blizzard conditions. He had brought gloves, a knit hat and an overcoat, but it was not enough. Lea had given him a wool scarf. He plunged ahead to the shopping center across the street. His feet got snowy and cold. The first refuge was a bagel shop. The enterprising entrepreneur had named it, Bagels and More. A steaming hot cup of coffee and a Danish restored his faith that all is well with the world.

Thinking of last night's awkward and frustrating rendezvous, he told himself, *you're expecting too much too fast. Remember, she's going through a trying time in her life. You've got to give her time to adjust. Be patient.* He sipped his coffee slowly, and reached into the inner recess of his mind. He plucked out a vivid memory of Nickie. And it reminded him of Lea—pressuring her, wanting her, just as before with Nickie.

CHAPTER THIRTEEN

Forty–two years ago Tom was struggling with his studies at Syracuse University. He had just gotten back from Europe and the horrors of World War II. He couldn't concentrate on the books, and studying was difficult. His interest was to forget the war, and to enjoy life.

Tom sat in the student union cafeteria smoking a cigarette and nursing a hangover. He was broke and couldn't even buy a cup of coffee. Through bleary eyes he saw Nickie walking into the cafeteria. She saw him and came over to his table.

"Hi. You don't look so good."

Tom looked up and smiled. "Guess you're right. I had one of those rousing nights with the boys last night. Nickie, would you take pity on a poor broke student and buy me a cup of coffee?"

"Sure. But you have to go and get it yourself. Here, take this dollar."

"Thank you. You're a life saver."

They had met four months earlier. Nickie's church youth group, of which she was president, came to Tom's church for an agreed upon reciprocal visit to each group's meeting. Later Tom brought his youth group to Nickie's church. Nickie had told him that her first name was Elizabeth, but liked to be called Nickie. Of course, that was derived from her last name.

"Nickie, I didn't know that you were a student here. It's good to see you."

"What are you studying?" She asked.

"Journalism. But I'm not doing very well. Can't seem to get back into the groove of being a student. I seem to be making up for lost time after the war. How about you. What course are you taking?"

"Just liberal art courses. I don't know what I want to do."

"You know, I'm not always the poor bedraggled soul that you see now. Remember, at our youth group meetings I was dressed decently and was clear eyed."

"I understand. We all have our bad days. Do you need another cup of coffee?"

"No thank you. Would you consider going out with me to a movie or for dinner? I'm not always broke you know. Could you go to dinner with me Saturday and then to my favorite bar?"

She looked at him and pictured how nice he looked all dressed up. He was a good looking man. She decided it would be nice to go out with Tom.

"I'd like that very much. What time will you come to my house?"

"Six o'clock. I have a special restaurant I'd like to take you to. We'll have an excellent dinner and then go to one of my favorite night spots for an after dinner drink."

Nickie rose from the table and said, "Sounds wonderful. I have a class now. See you Saturday night."

Tom said, "Thank you for saving my life this morning."

He watched as she glided smoothly between tables and out the door. She was as tall as he was. With straight back and head held high she was a beautiful lady. Her dignity was evident in the way she walked. She had long blonde hair, nearly golden in color, styled in a page–boy. She was elegant.

Dinner at Tobin's was as excellent as Tom had promised. He ordered for Nickie and himself. They toasted with glasses of Chablis. They talked of their studies at the university, their experiences with their respective church youth groups, and of their families.

As they left the restaurant, Nickie said, "That was a marvelous dinner. It was all you said it would be. Thank you, Tom."

"You're most welcome. Now, I'd like to take you to the little bar near here where my friends and I go after skiing. It's a friendly little neighborhood place. I'd like to show you off to my friends if they are there. You're a lovely lady and I would like to see you again soon."

Nickie was surprised. She wasn't expecting this approach of Tom's. It made her feel good. He was an interesting man. She wanted to know more about him.

"Do you mean you'd like to see me again in the student union, or some place more elegant?"

"Surely you can detect that I'd like to see you any time and place. I've been accused of wearing my heart on my sleeve and I think it shows now. I like you very much, Nickie."

"Thank you. I'd rather not go to your little bar tonight. I have an eight o'clock church meeting tomorrow, so I'd like to get home fairly early. However, I'd like to see you after skiing some time. Can you meet me in the student union Monday morning at ten o'clock?"

"I'll be there before ten waiting," Tom said.

Tom drove to her home where she lived with her parents and two sisters. They walked to the front door. He placed his hands on her shoulders and said, "I've had a wonderful time tonight Nickie." He kissed her lightly on the lips and said, "Thank you."

"It was a very nice evening for me too," she said softly. "See you Monday."

During six weeks of dates, Tom became more bold, more aggressive in his attempts to make love to Nickie. She was so alluring. Every day he told himself, I must have her.

Tom drove, at the end of the evening, to the water tower high on a hill overlooking the city. This was the lovers' rendezvous. There were three other cars there with occupants busily engaged in romantic pastimes. Tom and Nickie embraced eagerly. His roaming hands were not impeded. She was caught up in the romance of the moment and hungrily kissed him.

Their passion was overwhelming both of them. They kissed and hugged and sighed terms of endearment. Tom was looking forward to the ultimate ecstasy. Nickie could barely keep her passion in check. This was a lovely moment in their lives. Love and loving was imminent.

"Oh, Tom, please, I can't take this any more. I love you. I love you. But I can't go on this way. Let's come to our senses. Please." Nickie said.

Tom disengaged himself from her and looked penetratingly at her. " I know, I'm getting out of control, I'm too pushy, I'm rushing things. If there's love in me at all, it's for you. I don't know what love is. I haven't seen any of that for a long time. It just didn't exist over there in Europe. There was only war and hate, death and destruction. Oh God, I'm sorry."

"I think I understand. But it's over. You're home, you're here. The war is no more. Give yourself time and you'll forget."

"Yes, you're right. Time. The wasted time is over. You're here and that's all I care about. But it's difficult. You didn't see the bodies on Omaha Beach in Normandy, France. You didn't see the concentration camp at Dachau. You didn't hear our fighter pilot get shot down over the radio telephone. But you're right. I love you, Nickie. I want you to be my wife soon."

Tom felt that his coffee cup was cold. He came out of the reverie. He looked around the coffee shop and looked out the window. The still falling snow told him he was back in the present. He was in Columbus, Ohio.

CHAPTER FOURTEEN

The next two days in Columbus were both good and bad. It was good because Tom and Lea were together. They were beginning to know and understand each other. They genuinely appreciated each other's problems and the turmoil of their minds, and they each did their best to alleviate the doubts and the fears of the other. They talked at length of their past, and their hopes for the future. Their relationship seemed to be evolving from friendship to a deeper feeling for each other

It was bad because reticence, frustration, and the fear of going too far too soon caused them to skirt around the subject of a sexual encounter. Lea was still married. Tom had learned not to push too hard or too fast. The suppression of sexual desire was difficult, but he restrained himself. The week flew by quickly.

At the airport, waiting for Tom's flight to be called, they waited patiently and quietly, finding the right words difficult to express. Finally, close to departure time, Tom turned to Lea and took her hand in both of his.

"Lea, when I get home, I'll cool it. My letters won't be so frequent and I'll tone them down somewhat. I won't push or write such sexy phrases. Until your divorce is final, I guess we had better try to keep our distance both in thought and in attempting to see each other. Make no mistake about it, though, I want us to be together. We need each other, I'm sure."

"I think you're right. We need each other. There must be some kind of love beginning here. Thank you for being so understanding."

Tom's flight was called. They walked slowly to the gate, stopping short of the crowd. Tom turned to face Lea, set his one suitcase down, and put his arms around her. They held each other tightly and kissed passionately, disregarding the other travelers "Goodbye Lea. I hope everything works out for you soon and we can get together, preferably in Florida."

"Bye, T.J.. I hope so too. Au revoir. See I learned it."

"Very good." He waved as he disappeared through the gate.

During the flight back to Florida, Tom's thoughts were upsetting. *Why? Why do I have to endure this uncertainty? Why did God make us, all of us, insecure, with problems that at times seem insurmountable? Why can't life be rosy, easy, always happy? Because you have to prove you're strong, you can overcome doubt and adversity and troubles. That's as good an answer as I can think of.*

Then, in the core of his mind, he recalled overcoming adversity. That time in Belgium. The British truck hit his jeep. A deep gash in his head. Unconscious for a half hour. Waking up to see an angel of mercy with a wrinkled face, kind smiling eyes. The work–worn hands tending to my injury. She was an old Belgian farm housewife taking care of the liberator. I didn't conquer adversity. She did.

And then his air corps unit sent a B–26 bomber to get him and fly him back to the war in Germany. They solved his problem, and helped conquer the adversity, helped save my life along with an old woman.

So that's it. You don't do it alone. You're not isolated. There's always someone to help.

His thoughts rambled into a side tunnel of his brain, like the side tunnel in the mine thirteen hundred feet in the earth near Braunsweig, Germany. But I don't want to think about that. Get away from thoughts of war.

How did I become who I am? My mother and father molded me into a decent person, a gentleman. My friends, long ago, helped me evolve into the man of today. And the Air Force trained me to be an officer, to be responsible, to do the right thing in the circumstance of the moment.

You see, Tom, you don't solve problems alone. Someone has always been there to help.

You know damn well Lea will help. You've helped her. She'll see the right path. She'll take that path to you.

CHAPTER FIFTEEN

One of Lea's phone calls brought the good news that divorce proceedings were on track and the final decree would be soon.

Lea said excitedly, "the divorce will be final in early March next year. And my husband isn't contesting anything."

"Wonderful," Tom interjected, "but that's still four months away. I know, I'm too impatient."

"Yes. Remember patience is a virtue. The judge has set the court date as March 8th. That gives me time to wind up my affairs here. Thank goodness my children are with me on this decision. They approve of my attempt to build a new life."

"That's great. It's so nice to hear this good news. I'll write a letter tonight. See you, Lea. Love you."

"Yes. Love you, too. Bye."

That night, with his brain whirling, sleep would not come. His day started at three in the morning on the porch, listening to the night sounds. The frogs and toads were in rare form croaking raucously. It was as if one of them was the symphony conductor. At least fifty of the little creatures would start their night chorale in unison, and it would last for about thirty seconds.

In the background, always there but not always heard, were the crickets softly clicking their approval or disapproval of the frog and toad symphony.

Tom started a letter.

Dear Lea,

Your call today boosted my spirits tremendously. I expect you to be on an airplane March 9th. Where to? Only one place in the whole world—Florida.

Remember, lots of sunshine, no miserable winters, swimming in the pool every day, an occasional trip to the Officers' Club. Away from a sordid life to a new beginning with me—an officer and a gentleman who loves you...

Tom's thoughts turned back to Nickie. The doctor called Tom telling him to hurry over to the hospital. Nickie was failing quickly. Nothing could be done to stop the spread of cancer. He arrived just minutes after Nickie died. He stood looking at her for several minutes. The doctor and nurses stood quietly in the background. Tom leaned over and kissed Nickie's forehead. Then, quickly, he left the room with the doctor to make final arrangements.

As he opened the door to Nickie's father's house, Mr. Nichols was standing there looking apprehensive. Tom said, "Your daughter died peacefully at one forty–five." They immediately grasped one another in tight hugs and cryed. Their sobs echoed through the hallway but stopped suddenly as they regained their composure.

Tom's thoughts returned to the present. As he looked through the branches of the oak tree he saw the sun rising. *No,* he thought, *that's not possible. That's in the west.* My goodness, that's the full moon going down while the sun is shining on the east side of the house. He had never seen this phenomenon before.

Now's the time to finish the letter to Lea. I'll tell her amongst other things, about the moon and the sun.

CHAPTER SIXTEEN

Tom sat on the porch to read the letter from Lea that had just arrived.

Dear T. J.,

Here I go with some of my innermost thoughts. Please indulge me. I walked to the woods behind my daughter's house to my private place for meditation and a talk with God.

A soft late summer wind sifted through the trees ruffling my hair gently. I sat on the old fallen tree trunk at the edge of the woods, lifted my face to the sky and said, "Thank you, God for giving me hope, for giving me the wisdom to choose wisely."

The good early years are gone. The bad later years are gone. The new better years are coming soon. My mind drifted back to the early years of my marriage. I was in Canada on a fishing and camping trip with my husband and three children. Those were joyful days of swimming, fishing, hiking and teaching the children about nature and life.

"Look at this lovely woods flower. It's a trillium. And there is a beautiful Monarch butterfly. Isn't it nice and peaceful here away from the noisy city? Oh children, I love this outdoor life. I love you," I said to them.

I remembered too, my exhilaration at being the only one of the family that could get up on water skis behind the boat. The others tried and tried but failed. I was successful on my third attempt.

It was a great feeling, the feeling that I was the conquering hero. I could do anything. Those were lazy days, drifting in the boat fishing for our dinner. The languorous evenings by the fireplace reading or playing games with the family filled my heart with contentment and happiness.

For twenty years my life had been good. The next twenty years eroded into troubles, disappointments and failures. I don' t want to think of those days. But inexorably, into my mind, comes the greatest disappointment of my life. My twenty–fifth wedding anniversary celebration had been planned for months. My husband and I were going to Hawaii. Two weeks before departing my husband informed me, "I don't want to go. I'm not going."

Stunned at this pronouncement, I tried in vain to change his mind. How can he do this to me, I had thought. Finally, I gave up and invited a girl friend to go with me. We had a wonderful, exciting time. But I never got over the unforgivable disappointment my husband had caused.

My thoughts come back to today now. A gust of warm wind stirs the leaves at my feet, whirling them round and round. "Thank you, summer wind, for getting me out of the bad years memory," I said aloud to the wind, the trees, myself.

I looked across the field and saw an old man plodding slowly along the dirt road. His long gray hair was rumpled by the wind. His bent back and slow pace seemed to tell the story of a hard life. I'm really lucky, I thought. I'm reasonably healthy. A bad knee and a failed marriage, but there's you. Seventy year old T.J., eight years older than I. But you look and act younger than I. Somehow we're meant for each other.

But how can I leave my children? I'll be a thousand miles away from them. Even though they have their own lives, their own families, I won't see them often. Oh God, why must we mortals have to contend with such problems. Remember, I said to myself, you've made your choice, your decision. You know in your heart it's right. More and more, as the day's go too slowly by, I'm sure I need you, and you need me.

I rose from my place at the edge of the woods and walked briskly and confidently back to the house.

CHAPTER SEVENTEEN

Tom slept late. It was eight o'clock in the morning when he crawled out of bed. A long stretch of his body to loosen the old joints, a gaping yawn, and he was ready for another day. While starting to dress, he heard desperate screams for help. They were coming from behind his house.

"Help, help me."

He dressed quickly and raced out the back door. The screams had subsided. He looked at the house behind his. There were four women clustered together beside the swimming pool. One of them was crying hysterically. He ran to the swimming pool and the distraught women.

"What's wrong?" he asked.

"I tried. I really did. I did." Jean babbled and sobbed.

The other women were gathered around Jean trying to calm her. Tom looked around and saw Jean's seven year old son lying on the deck motionless. He hurried to the boy who was lying in a wet spot on the deck. A trail of water led from there to the pool. The boy had been under water too long. Not knowing CPR procedure, Tom started the old fashioned artificial respiration. He kneeled over the small body and pressed on his back.

"I tried. He was at the bottom of the deep end. Oh God, I tried. I can't swim so I pushed him to the shallow end with the brush on the long pole. Then I got him out."

"Have you called an ambulance or the police?" Tom asked.

"Yes, the rescue squad." Jean answered.

Impatiently Tom said, "Have you tried CPR?"

"He's dead. What can we do?" Jean replied.

Tom bent to his task. As he pressed on the little back a spurt of water came from the boy's mouth and he felt a slight shudder in the child's body. He continued pressing.

The ambulance crew came running from the side of the house into the pool area. They quickly went to the boy. Tom moved as one of the rescue attendants took over and started CPR.

Tom went to Jean and clasped one of her hands. "I think he'll make it. I got some water out of him."

"Thank you. I didn't know what to do."

"Why didn't one of the other women start CPR or artificial respiration?"

"We thought it was too late. We thought he was dead."

One of the ambulance crew shouted, "We've got vital signs. Pretty good ones. Think he'll be okay. Come on guys, let's get him to the hospital."

"Oh, thank God." Jean sighed as she hurried to the stretcher and clasped one of her son's hands. His eyes opened slightly and Jean smiled.

Tom quietly left Jean's home and trudged back to his home. He sank into the chaise on the porch and thought about what had happened. Surely one of the four women should have had the presence of mind to do something. Hope Jean's son will be okay.

Lea would have had the presence of mind to do something. She'd start CPR. I know she would handle an emergency quickly.

CHAPTER EIGHTEEN

Dear Lea,

Your call today boosted my spirits tremendously. I expect you to be on an airplane March 9th. Where to? Only one place in the whole world—Florida.

Remember—lots of sunshine, no miserable winters, swimming in the pool every day, and an occasional trip to the Officers' Club. Away from a sordid life to a new beginning with me—an officer and a gentleman who loves you. I know, you've heard this before.

My rambling thoughts always focus on you, us, our personal traumas, our meeting. We were like two lost ships on the sea of uncertainty and despair. We drifted somehow to the same island, the island of our love.

Just think, what unexpected chance brought us together. Our train times could have been different, routes different. So many variables could have kept us floating aimlessly and not finding each other.

The random thoughts keep coming, and I like to express them to you. Perhaps they will help you to understand the type of man you're getting involved with. Why this one came to mind I don't know.

A chance remark by a young friend of mine indicated that he thought people my age had little or no interest in sex. We were too old to be interested sexually, and even could not perform the sex act. I wonder how he got the idea that sex was only for the young and middle age people. Little does he know. If he knew what you and I know about sexual relations, his life, I am sure, would be fuller and more satisfying.

There I go again, but this time it's a bit of philosophy coming forth. Not prodding you to think of our sexual life to come.

And the random rambling goes on. It's good to get these thoughts out of my brain. It's a release, a purging of my mind to get these thoughts out and into words to you.

Enough! I've unloaded enough of my rambling on you. It's time to end this river of thoughts. I don't want to bore you. When we get together the river will flow again.

Love you,
T.J.

CHAPTER NINETEEN

The days were getting short. The days were also long waiting for Lea. It's a long, long time from September to November and on to March.

In November, a phone call provided respite from the drudgery of his lonely life. It was Bud, his life–long friend in Syracuse, New York.

"Tom, how ya doin'?"

"I'm fine. And you?"

"Great. Just have to be careful with my diabetes. My wife and I have the fabulous idea of having a reunion of us four old buddies, Rod, Hank, you and I here at my house. We're thinking of two weeks from now, the 16th. Hank will already be here. I'll just have to call Rod. Can you make it?"

"Sure. You know I'm foot loose and fancy free these days. I'll be there. I'll stay at my sister's apartment. I'll be there the 15th and call you."

"Okay, Tom. Dinner at my house the 16th. See you."

"So long, Bud."

Bud, Tom, Rod and Hank had been together through their college years and up to the beginning of World War II. Then, of course, they had gone their separate ways. All four had gone into the Army or the Air Corp. Rod from Pittsburgh, Hank from California, and Tom from Florida. The date had been set. There was nothing to keep Tom from making it to this grand affair. On November fifteenth, Tom flew to

Syracuse and was able to stay at his sister's apartment. He also had the use of her car.

The next day all four of the old friends and three wives met at Bud's house for dinner. But Tom didn't let Nickie's absence bother him. She was in his thoughts as he proposed the first toast. Rod prematurely chimed in that, "Tom will drink to anything."

"To Nickie. A wonderful, caring, lovely mother, wife and companion for forty–two years." They all raised their glasses, silently thinking of Nickie.

To relieve the tension, Tom said, "Now, let's have a toast proposed by one of you for the brightness of the future."

It wasn't long before the conversation turned to remembrances of the old days. The four boys listening to big band records in Hank's room above the garage, kept time with the beat of the music by tapping their feet. They soaked up the sounds of Benny Goodman, Glen Miller, Tommy Dorsey, and many other bands. They turned back to their college days at Syracuse University—drinking beer by the pitcher at the Hafermaltz beer parlor. They remembered bitching about the early eight o'clock classes with hangovers, coffee and cigarettes in the Student Union cafeteria, Cafe Garzone on the South side of town listening to jukebox records and swilling beer. Those were good times.

The next evening they all met at a restaurant for a sumptuous dinner, wine, cocktails and more toasts. As usual, Tom had veal Oscar.

The day after, they all went their separate ways. Tom got his flight to Florida and was home by five o'clock.

The inexorable languorous days trudging through the week, the seemingly unending saunter of weeks to the end of a month was an all too grim reality. The days were empty. It was a time when Tom's "cup runneth under." Jules had created this phrase in one of his stories. Jules was an architect whose avocation was writing. When he died, Tom gave an eulogy to Jules, using his "cup runneth under" phrase to compliment his writing skill. The cup of days were not only empty but sometimes seemed to be interminably long. Loneliness and long, drawn–out days were interspersed with family get–togethers at Thanksgiving, Christmas and New Year celebrations. The longest days were filled with yearning and thoughts of Lea.

CHAPTER TWENTY

After an enjoyable breakfast of a Belgian waffle at Johnnie's restaurant and banter with his favorite waitress, Nancy. Tom returned home and sat down to do some writing. His plan was to write at least three hundred words, edit it, rewrite it and edit it again. At the two hundred word mark he took a break and looked out the window. The mail had arrived. He knew there would be a letter from Lea.

.   .   .

Dear T.J.,

The snow is laying softly on the tree limbs, sparkling like diamonds in the bright moonlight. What a beautiful sight. Would I miss this if I go to Florida to be with you? How would I cope with being away from the children and lifelong friends?

I'm sitting here in my office watching the snow blowing ominously outside. It's starting to drift. Brr. I need a warm body to cuddle up to, namely T.J.. Oh, there I go with the inner thoughts that I believed I could never voice.

I'm doing things and harboring thoughts I've never done before. And the good part is that I don't feel guilty about it. So, this tells me I have severed the cord that has tied me to the past, and I'm looking forward to a "new life" of happiness with you. My Dad always said, "Good things are worth waiting for." I really want to be with you—to make you happy, to be your companion, and to be your lover.

As I stare at the drifting snow, my thoughts go back to the Lake Shore Limited. Why would you choose me, out of all the people you met, to bare your soul to? Why did I take your telephone number? Why did I confide in you? I still feel we were brought together for a special reason. I felt your warmth and love and caring just in those few hours we had together on the train.

Now for the really big news. Just think. I'll be free on March ninth and we can be together.

I'll mail this letter today but I won't be able to keep this milestone news to myself waiting for your reply. I've got to call you this evening.

See you soon.

LOVE, ETC.,
Lea

After sealing the envelope, she leaned back in her chair and peered out the window. The snowflakes were drifting down lazily now and the wind had subsided. Her thoughts drifted again to the Lake Shore Limited. T.J. had eased her troubled mind. He had shown her that a new, happy life was possible. He was beginning to develop a new life. She should be able to do the same.

•   •   •

As he sat there listening to Mantovani and reminiscing, thoughts of Nickie were shunted into the background and Tom's memory came forward to the days of the Lake Shore Limited and Lea. As if on cue, the telephone rang and he sensed that it would be his second love.

"Hello, Tom here."

"Hi, Lea here in Cleveland away from you. I have earthshaking, major news for you. You better be lounging in your chaise so you won't collapse on the floor."

"Wow! That world–shaking and momentous! Okay, I'm ready. Go ahead with your startling news bulletin."

"I'll be there on March tenth. I've written a letter to you giving all the details. Isn't that great? Now we can be together. My old life is closed, and a new life with you is about to begin. Will you be at the airport to meet me?"

"I'll be there with bells on. Wonderful. You are so right—earthshaking. Oh Lea, it's finally happening. I can't believe it, but yes, I can believe it. This is the way it is supposed to be."

"I have lots to do to get ready and wind up my things here. I'm so happy. I'm free to be with you. Have to go now. The letter is in the mail. See you in about four weeks. And I'll be there with bells on too. Love you. Bye."

"Love you too, Lea. This is wonderful. Bye."

CHAPTER TWENTY ONE

The pilot "greased" the big jet onto the runway. The wheels barely screeched as the big bird touched down. The white knuckles of the young girl next to Lea began to return to a pinkish flesh color. Lea smiled to herself and inwardly wanted to shout "Hooray, at last I'm here! T.J., I'm here."

The sleek silver aircraft trundled up to the terminal gate and stopped. Lea was the first to jump up out of her seat. It was exasperating: the slow progress of the people.

As she left the jet–way and entered the terminal, she immediately saw T.J. He was in blue slacks, blue shirt and with bells on. A little cluster of three bells hung from his shirtfront. Lea ran to him and dropped her luggage. They hugged and kissed oblivious to the stares and smiles of the other travelers.

"Lea, it has finally happened. You're here. No more awful waiting. We can be together for those precious few days."

"Oh T.J., isn't it wonderful. I love you. I love the bells," she said smiling, her eyes twinkling.

"They ring out for you. I love you, Lea. I've missed you so. Come. We'll get your luggage then head for home. Listen to that. Home, our home. What wonderful, musical words."

On the drive to Tom's home they talked excitedly of their happiness, their plans for the future, their new golden days of living.

That evening they talked for hours, Tom told Lea of his plans and ideas for the immediate future. Lea agreed and was amazed that his thoughts were hers too. Most surprising and unexpected was his plan for them to go to Normandy, France.

"I want to revisit Omaha Beach, the site of D–Day landings In World War II. I was there in 1944 during the invasion."

Lea said, "That should be a wonderful trip." She had never done any traveling overseas. It would be exciting to see a foreign country. But, they were too consumed with the moments of the present to talk about details of that trip.

The days and weeks were filled with excitedly finding out more about each other   their dreams, their hopes, their preferences. It was too cold to swim in the unheated pool, so they walked the beach. Early one morning, they arrived early enough to see the sun rise from out of the ocean, the orange globe springing from the horizon. They walked hand in hand along the hard packed sand and relished their togetherness.

The nights were consumed with more exploring of each other, and with love. The thoughts expressed in letters became sublime reality.

The months passed by quickly as they enjoyed their life with each other. Lea flew to Cleveland to see her children and to drive her car down to Florida loaded with some of her personal things.

A drive to the Officers' Club at Patrick Air Force Base for dinner and dancing was a highlight of their getting to know each other. They melded together on the dance floor as if they had been enjoying it for years. After a gracious and delicious dinner they went to the lounge where windows overlooked the ocean and they could see the gantries at the Kennedy Space Center. A shuttle was being readied for launch. They sipped their brandy alexanders and watched the ships and sailboats on the horizon. Tom introduced Lea to Sam, the bartender, and told Lea of the flight nurse after seeing the wings on Sam's vest. They danced away the remainder of the evening, then headed for their home.

CHAPTER TWENTY TWO

It was a hot, humid evening. Lea was late as usual for the divorce support group meeting in Doctor Lane's office.

"I better call Sandy to let her know I'll be late," Lea said to T.J. "She'll be wondering what happened."

"Why can't you program your time more efficiently and not be late so often." T.J. smiled. "The Air Force would have straightened you out."

"We're not all as prompt and organized as you, colonel," she snapped as she put on her gold earrings. "Sandy will understand."

Lea called Sandy. Then she kissed T.J. goodbye and rushed out the door. Now what? The car wouldn't start. Frustrated, she called to T.J., "My car won't start. Can I take yours?"

"All right," he replied. "Be careful, it's my pet."

. . . .

While driving to Sandy's house, Lea's mind was whirling. *Being divorced was not as easy as I anticipated,* she thought. There were so many adjustments, guilt feelings and unexpected problems. Lucky for me that I had nurse's training so that finding work was not an obstacle.

Sandy was a true friend and a great support. They met at Doctor Lane's counseling sessions. Together they had gone through counseling and retreats. The hurt and humiliation of a divorce was difficult to heal.

Lea blew the horn three times at Sandy's house. In acknowledgement Sandy flashed the porch light three times. Sandy looked great in her gray suit, pink silk blouse and a gold band around her head as she got into the *brown bomber,* the nickname for T.J.'s 1973 Pontiac.

"Hi. I see you have the big bomber tonight. Car trouble again?" Sandy remarked.

"(Yes. Always something going wrong. Wow, losing weight becomes you, Sandy. The new exercise regimen is working for you. Wish I could get motivated," Lea moaned.

"You will. It takes time," smiled Sandy. She always had a consoling answer.

Everyone was busy discussing their problems by the time they arrived. It was a small room with a couch and several chairs arranged in a circle so the group could communicate easily.

"Sorry we're late. I had car trouble," Lea said apologetically.

Mary began to tell how her husband came home one night, packed his bags and left. She had no idea that her husband was thinking of leaving. This was an example of stories heard at the meeting. Everyone there was a *dumpee,* an expression used to identify your status in a divorce. Everyone except Lea. She was a *dumper,* and had filed for the divorce. When Lea's turn came to talk she told the group how she missed the companionship of her daughters. The phone bills were piling up. But she had to accept the barrier of distance. It was her choice to leave Ohio and come to Florida to live with T.J.

Sandy's situation was different. Her husband left for a younger woman. She had known nothing of his philandering.

Later, Lea told of the guilt, how difficult it was to exist living with a stranger in his home, surrounded with his deceased wife's belongings. "It was more wrenching than I had imagined," she said. "Leaving every-thing—my family, friends and my hometown was painful. What possessed me to do it during the trauma of the divorce? My reasoning was impaired by emotions and desires. It was T.J.'s persuasion of a better life with him.

His charm and understanding, his encouraging letters had prompted me to be adventurous," she told the group. The girls were impressed that there was hope for them to meet someone after their pain healed.

After the meeting everyone went to Denny's to socialize.

On the way home Lea's mind drifted back to Cleveland, to Charleton, a widower, a dear friend from her early years of marriage. He was a quiet, homebody type of man. His deceased wife had been her best friend since childhood. After she had decided on divorce and was living with her daughter, Charleton began to pursue her. Lea thought of the time she went to dinner with him.

"Lea, button up your overcoat. You'll catch cold."

The wind was howling around her head as they got into his car. The snow glistened in the lights.

"The dinner was fantastic, Charleton. I've never been to the 100th Bomb Group restaurant. It was the nostalgic atmosphere of a World War II bomb shelter, and the big band music was wonderful."

Charleton smiled lovingly at Lea. "Thought you'd like it. It's a favorite place of mine. Reminds me of the days when I was in the army. Lea, lets go to my house for a bit, light the fire in the fireplace and have a drink. My son, Phil, won't be home 'till late. He's staying with me since his divorce. We can reminisce and dance to the Glen Miller band. My collection of tapes is endless."

"Okay. Glen Miller is one of my favorite bands. Do you have his 'In the Mood'"

There was a cold silence as Charleton drove to his house. He kept glancing over at Lea wondering what she was thinking. As they drove into the garage and parked the car, Charleton leaned over and kissed her softly on the lips.

"Lea," he said nervously, "After my wife died I knew that I loved you. Now that we are free we can get together. Am I being too presumptuous?"

Stunned and surprised at his aggressiveness Lea was perplexed. Recovering some measure of composure, she said, in a quivering voice,

"I never dreamed you felt this way about me. I always thought of you as a dear friend, Charleton. You know I'm deeply involved with T.J."

"Yeah, but he's in Florida. And it won't last," he said angrily. "Meeting on a train, how ridiculous. We've known each other for thirty–five years. We're meant for each other."

Lea felt tears coming to her eyes. "All I wanted was a friendly relationship. How can we be lovers? Your wife was my best friend since we were sixteen. No! It's impossible. I'm in love with T.J. Please, take me home."

A truck horn blaring loudly brought her back from her reverie into the present. But still she reflected, it was nice to be wanted. It was like being back in high school and Queen of the Prom. But I'm sixty–two, she thought, not eighteen.

The days grow short as we reach September rang in her ears. Our song, T.J.'s and mine. He's such a romantic. It was heavenly being spoiled, she thought, and deep down she felt it was right. God put him into my life for a purpose, she said to herself. He's an angel, here to guide and help me. Our meeting on AMTRAK was God's will for both of us. We are so compatible and he is so comforting. Enjoy him. Enjoy this life. Listen to your heart. You love him, Lea kept telling herself.

CHAPTER TWENTY THREE

Tom said, "It's time to do some investigating and planning, Lea. Time is a fleeting thing. We have to plan for our trip to Normandy, France. Specifically, to Omaha Beach at the village of Vierville sur Mer."

"You're right. I feel ready to go right now. I've never traveled outside the United States. What are your ideas so far?"

"Well, I'm a charter member of the Battle of Normandy Foundation. I've donated to the building of their museum in Caen, France. The foundation has commissioned a travel agency to plan and execute a tour of Normandy—the beaches, the battlegrounds, the cemeteries, and of course their museum. There's an advertisement for it in my Retired Officer Magazine. I'll show it to you."

"I'm excited about going to France. Will we go to England also?"

"Yes, England first then across the English channel to Cherbourg and down the peninsula to Normandy. I'm going to write for the details of the tour plan right away and see how much it costs."

Two weeks later the important documents came in the mail. Tom read them carefully, then pointed out the highlights to Lea. They would leave Miami on British Air on June 2nd next year and return ten days later. The itinerary would take them to all the villages, beaches and cemeteries that Tom wanted to see. Paris was also on the itinerary. Lea was excited at the prospect.

The following months were filled with work and play. Lea was busy two days a week with her job as a Licensed Practical Nurse. She took care of an eighty–two year old gentleman who had emphysema. Tom was busy with his meetings, teaching contract bridge and of course writing. Lea did most of the grocery shopping.

They went out occasionally to dinner—Ocean Grill, La Fonda, and the Officers' Club. Lea was getting acclimated to the weather of Florida. They swam every day and some evenings in their pool.

They were almost constantly anxious and looking forward to June. As May approached they began to plan the clothes to take on the trip to Normandy. They had their passports, insurance, badges from the Department of Defense, and had accomplished all required paperwork. They were ready and eager to go.

CHAPTER TWENTY FOUR

It was good to settle down into routine daily life. Lea and Tom frolicked in the pool every afternoon just before the four o'clock cocktail hour.

They had purchased a personal computer and printer so Tom's writing was easier now, that is, the mechanical part. The words and phrases sometimes flowed easily, but occasionally had to be slowly dredged up. Their life together was more than happy. It was satisfying and rewarding in every way.

On a hot afternoon in mid–July sitting on the patio, vodka and orange juice in hand after a refreshing swim, Tom said, "Lea, I've been doing some thinking. The old brain has been whirling. A phrase said by Eugene Ionesco, a playwright I think, that I can't get out of my mind. He said, 'We haven't the time to take our time.' How true. The same as in "September Song" that sings, 'But the days grow short when you reach September. One hasn't got time for the waiting game.'"

"My goodness. Your brain really is in high gear. I love your reference to our song."

"Yes. Anyway," Tom continued, "remember, One Hundred Club dances start in November. I told you about that Club. I'd like to get a new jacket for this season. Maybe a green one. And I imagine you'd like a new dress. So, how about going tomorrow to Palm Beach and see what we find?"

80

"Amazing," Lea answered, "Two great minds on the same trail of thought. I've been thinking about a new dress too. Sounds wonderful going to Palm Beach. I want to check Petite Sophisticates at the mall too."

"Roger, as we say in the Air Force. Know what that means?"

"Sure. It means okay, I understand."

"Right. You're brilliant."

In Palm Beach they found Tom's expensive green jacket, and the smooth salesman produced the necktie that matched perfectly.

On the way home they stopped at the mall to check Petite Sophisticates for a dress. Lea chose a red dress that looked exquisite on her. While they were shopping a dressy pantsuit caught Tom's eye. It looked beautiful on Lea but the beige color did nothing to enhance her complexion and hair.

They left the mall and on the way home stopped for a cocktail. They ordered two brandy alexanders, Lea's favorite drink. Tom couldn't get the beige pantsuit out of his mind.

"Lea, that beautiful beige pant suit that wasn't you brought to mind a similar pant suit that Nickie wore. It was the same color, almost the hue of raw silk."

"What did it look like? Can you describe it?"

"I'm not too good at this but I'll try. The pant legs were full, so full they nearly looked like a dress. The waist was form–fitting with an attached belt that served only as a decorative element. This was a one–piece suit, not to be confused with a modern jump suit. The top was full, slightly bloused, with a V–neck. Not a plunging neck line but a little provocative. The sleeves were long and full. Around the neckline and down to the waist was lacy material the same raw silk color that accented the bosom. She looked stunning in it. Does that picture it for you?"

"It sure does. You should be writing copy for women's dress shop advertisements."

"Thanks. There doesn't seem to be pants suits like that now days. You'd look great in that style but a different color. Perhaps a light blue or British racing green."

"Racing green is too dark. It'd have to be a lighter green, perhaps Kelly green. I wish we could find it."

"Yes, that would be nice."

Tom continued. "We bought that pant suit before I went to Newfoundland. Nickie and the kids came up later when housing became available. At the Air Base Officers' Club we had many parties and dances. Lots of baby sitters were available so we went to the club often. There was a Navy base there too so we also had the use of their club."

"Wow. You must have had a busy social life there."

"Yes, but I was on shift duty and couldn't be at all dances and parties. Anyway, it was there that I learned a big lesson about married life. At the two clubs parties, I began paying too much attention to other officer's wives. Too often I left Nickie and danced with other ladies. At a New Year's Eve party at the Navy club, I suddenly noticed that Nickie wasn't there. So I went looking for her. To me, she was the most beautiful lady there in her beige pantsuit. I was worried. Anyway, I finally found her in a dark, unused room sitting on a sofa with a big, handsome Navy pilot, a Lieutenant Commander. I calmly told her it was time to leave. She hesitated briefly, said goodbye to the officer, and came to join me. We went back home in silence. The kids were asleep. Then, I blew up. I even grabbed her roughly and berated her for getting too cozy with the Navy pilot. It was then that I learned my lesson. Nickie told me how left out and unwanted she felt when I was playing with other officer's wives. She said she didn't really want to do it, but decided what's good for the goose is also good for the gander. So she went off alone with the Navy officer. I saw the light, told her I loved her, and promised to be more attentive. The tender "mad love" was exotic that night. There you have it—the story behind the beige pant suit."

"I'm glad you learned that lesson long ago. Now you're not a butterfly flitting from flower to flower, right?"

"You're right, my dear. No more flitting around."

CHAPTER TWENTY FIVE

Lea completed a lap of side stroke in the pool and stood in the shallow end watching Tom. He was doing his pool exercises. The one he was doing now stretched the lower back muscles and seemed to keep him reasonably supple and limber. In chest deep water, his back against the side of the pool, he swung each leg with knees bent to the opposite side of his body. They looked at each other, admiring what they saw. Lea was beautiful in her flowered swim suit, while Tom was muscular and hairy chested in his briefs.

"Okay Tom, now the toe touching exercise and you'll be raring to go tonight."

"You're a hard task master, Lea. But you're right. I have to try to keep this ancient body in good shape. Let me see you do the backstroke now. I love to see your two hills bobbing around in the water like two buoys marking the location of my treasure." He laughed wickedly.

"Oh, you old lecher." And off she went on a lap of backstroke.

As he watched admiringly, standing at the side of the pool, he heard the sound of a helicopter approaching. As it came into view he saw that it was an Air Force craft, a big one. It looked like one he was familiar with. "Lea, look there, just coming over the oak tree. It's a big chopper like the one I was in up in Newfoundland."

"I see it Tom. What's this about Newfoundland? That's one I haven't heard yet."

"That's another story I have to tell. Some day I'll write it. The punch line of the story is that the helicopter took off while I was hanging on to the outside of the chopper. I let go and fell about six feet to the ground unhurt."

"You sure had some harrowing experiences. Tell me, were you eager to retire when you did? Was it good to get away from Air Force duty and the hazardous situations?"

"I was ready to retire. In my business, radar operations, I couldn't go much farther up the ladder of promotions. Also, in that field of duty I was too vulnerable to being sent to isolated assignments where the family could not accompany me. I had had enough of that. But enough of the past. I'm looking forward to the future, the immediate future of us together playing in bed."

"As I've said before, you're an old lecher."

After Lea finished frolicking and flirting with T.J. in the pool, she slithered out of the water to relax in the sun. The sky was a deep shade of blue and cloudless. It was perfect. Lea got comfortable on a lounge chair to soak up the wonderful Florida sun. Here one could really relax and enjoy the summer ocean breeze which came in from the shore every afternoon.

"T.J. could you please apply some suntan lotion on my back?" called Lea. "It's almost cocktail hour and I want to rest awhile."

"I'll be right over," T.J. responded. He loved to massage lotion all over Lea.

As he applied the lotion, Lea cooed, "Oh, that feels so good."

T.J. leaned over and kissed her gently on the softest lips in the world.

"Be careful or we'll end up in the bedroom." Lea said.

"Not a bad idea," T.J. replied.

"Maybe after our cocktails and a shower," Lea responded sensuously. "I want to sun bathe for a while. Love you."

T.J. abided by her wishes reluctantly. After their cocktails was a nice consolation.

The healing rays of the sun were beginning to penetrate her body and Lea became relaxed. She loved the pool. This had always been a dream of hers, to have one and swim at her leisure. She thanked God for her blessings.

Lea's train of thought was interrupted by T.J. calling, "It's cocktail hour. What would you desire, my lady."

Leisurely sipping their drinks on the porch, savoring every minute with each other, they toasted.

"To your health," T.J. offered.

"To our health," Lea countered.

CHAPTER TWENTY SIX

The phone rang as Lea and Tom were doing dishes in the kitchen. Tom, nearest to the telephone took the call.

"Hello. Tom Kelley Here."

"Elizabeth please," the caller said abruptly.

"For you Lea."

She took the phone. "Elizabeth. Hello." She listened intently for a few seconds. "No, oh God no." Her agonized scream brought Tom to her side. Tears streamed down her cheeks as she clung tightly to the counter top. Again, she listened as she sobbed. Lea could not speak and she collapsed against Tom. He listened to the phone and heard only dial tone. With arms around her, he led her to the sofa as she sobbed. "What is it Lea? What has happened?"

"Oh Tom, Betty is dead. My daughter Betty. She was shot. My beautiful Betty, only thirty–eight years old, was killed."

"I'm so sorry. How did it happen?"

"No details were given. She was killed instantly by a bullet to her head. My Betty, my child is dead. Betty's father–in–law called. It was a cold unthoughtful call with no expression of sympathy. All he said was 'Betty is dead. She was shot,' and he hung up."

"You'll have to fly to Cleveland right away. I'll call Bill to get a flight as soon as possible."

"Yes, okay. No, I'm so confused. I need to call James and Diana to tell them the horrible news. Oh Tom, what will I do without Betty? We were so close." She sobbed softly.

As Tom reached for the phone to punch in the numbers for Lea, the phone rang. Tom took the call.

"Hello. The Kelley residence," Tom answered.

"Hi, this is Harry in Cleveland. I'm a friend of Lea 's. Jack, Betty's husband asked me to call and explain the accident to you. He's too devastated to talk about it. I'm so sorry. Betty was the victim of a freak accident on the Willoughby farm at an annual picnic. The gang of two dozen friends meet every year and they have a shooting range set up there. Bill, Jack's best friend was at the firing line. His gun jammed. As he tried to clear it at the table behind him the gun fired and the bullet went into the group of women standing nearby, striking only Betty who died instantly from a bullet to her head."

Tom listened intently. "Thank you for calling. I'll tell Lea." He hung up the phone, turned to Lea, and told her what Harry had said.

"What am I going to do?" Lea sobbed. "I have to call my son and my daughter. Oh God, why, why!"

"I'll call your daughter and son if you want me to."

"No. I'll do it. Jut give me a few minutes. Betty is gone. Oh Tom, what a horrid way to die."

"Thank God she died instantly and felt no pain."

Lea finally got the courage to call James and Diana to tell them of their sister's death. Tom called the travel agent and booked a non–stop flight the next afternoon. Tom had too many obligations to be able to accompany Lea to Cleveland.

"I'll be staying at my sister Lou's house in Cleveland. I'll call you as soon as I learn more of what happened."

Tom drove Lea to the West Palm Beach airport in the late afternoon. He consoled Lea until her flight was called, then he hugged her tightly and gently kissed her. "Try to be strong, my love. It must be awful losing a child. Your sister will help you through this trying time. I love you."

"I wish you could come with me. But I know it would be awkward for both of us with my ex–husband there. Bye. I love you." Even as a tear or two rolled onto her cheeks, she held her head high as she entered the jetway.

• • •

Two days after arriving in Cleveland Lea called Tom. In halting phrases she described the details of how Betty had been killed.

"The police have already completed a preliminary investigation. They have talked to Bill the man who held the gun, and also to Betty's husband and several of the witnesses. The absence of normal safety precautions at the shooting range were obvious to the Portage County Sherrif's Department authorities."

"Bill, the shooter should never have turned around at the firing line with his .44 caliber Magnum revolver in hand. He should have faced the target area while trying to unload spent shells. The revolver was a six shot weapon. Only five shots had been fired and there was one left in the chamber. Also, there was no supervisor at the firing line to enforce safety regulations. The key word voiced by a sherrif's deputy was negligence. The shooter was negligent and attention to safety was negligent."

Tom replied, "Sure does sound like a case of negligence. I wonder if Bill will be charged?"

"The Sherrif's Department has not charged him yet. Betty's funeral service and burial will be tomorrow. At the funeral my sister will give a eulogy. The eulogy will be a poem written by Betty about ten years ago. It's beautiful. I'd like to read it to you."

Lea continued in a quivering voice.

A Special Blessing

"Happiness can't be defined. It's a certain mood, a state of mind. It's sharing everyday affairs with someone who understands and cares. It's a tender look or a gentle touch that says, 'I love you very much.'

There was a long silence and Tom could hear Lea quietly weeping. Then she continued.

It's a smile of welcome when you're blue, a dream that's shared, a dream for two. And happiness, it's more than this—a warm embrace and a magic kiss. It's a special blessing from above. It's what I have when I'm in love."

"Isn't it a lovely poem? She was a talented daughter in many ways. I loved her so much."

"Yes Lea. The poem's marvelous and perfect as a tribute to Betty."

"I'm bearing up under the strain. As you once said, death is final. It has to be accepted even though it's so sad and traumatic." She paused. "I'll call you the day after tomorrow with my return schedule. Have to go. Love you Tom."

"Love you too. Bye Lea."

CHAPTER TWENTY SEVEN

Three weeks after Lea came back home Tom made the big decision. It had to be done right and he knew how to do it.

"Let's have dinner in the dining room for a change. I'll set it up on your beautiful lace tablecloth. I'll use one of our centerpieces and two tall white candles. And of course the best china and silverware" Tom suggested.

"What's the special occasion?" Lea asked.

"Nothing special. I just thought it'd be nice for a change, a semblance of formality. I know you're planning to have sirloin steaks tonight. And we'll have burgundy wine for our toast."

"Sounds wonderful, even exotic. I'll make sure I do the steaks just right."

They first toasted each other with their favorite French toast. Lea had prepared a marvelous dinner. They savored every bite. Just before dessert Tom proposed another toast "To us and long happy lives."

As they put down their glasses, Lea said, "You seem to be edgy. Is something wrong?"

"No, everything is fine, in fact couldn't be better. It's just that I'm anxious to give you a little something." He reached under the table and retrieved a gift. "For you my dear. Because I love you."

"T.J. how nice. What is it?"

"I forget. Open it and find out."

"You rascal," she purred as she unwrapped the gift. As she opened the small box, Lea saw the beautiful diamond ring.

"Oh, it's beautiful. I love the marquis cut of the stone. It's a lovely dinner ring."

Before she could say any more, Tom said lovingly, "It's not a dinner ring, it's your engagement ring. Will you marry me?"

"Oh T.J.," beaming she replied, "Yes. Yes! I'm so happy. I love you so much."

They leaned to each other and kissed passionately.

"Now for the piece de resistance. Engagement by itself is wonderful, but not enough. There is something missing. Just like after marriage there is the honeymoon, after the engagement there must be a consummation, especially in our case."

"Oh oh," Lea murmured. "What is that fertile mind of yours devising now?"

"I have already made reservations for the creme de la creme of all engagement celebrations for second time around lovers like us. We are going to a bed and breakfast home."

CHAPTER TWENTY EIGHT

The Mellon Patch is located on North Hutchinson Island a little North of Fort Pierce, Florida on route A1A. It is on the Indian River side of the road at the end of a canal which connects to the river. It is a new bed and breakfast house, built specifically for that purpose.

Lea and T.J. paused at the front door admiring the high vaulted ceiling they could see inside.

"How light and cozy it is there with a fireplace for the cool winter days. It's beautifully decorated in light Florida colors," Lea admired.

"Yes, it's very attractive."

Andrea, innkeeper of the Patch, welcomed then. "Come in. You are the Kelleys I presume. I'll show you around and you can choose which room you want."

There were only four guestrooms and Lea chose the Seascape room on the second floor. A mermaid–shaped pillow graced the bed. A small balcony overlooked the spacious back patio, lawn, canal and river. It was an idyllic and tranquil setting.

They dressed for dinner and drove to a waterfront restaurant in Vero Beach. Back at the Mellon Patch they sat in rocking chairs on the patio admiring the moonlit scene before them. The moonlight glowed on the canal water.

Their bonding that evening was slow, deliberate and amorous. They reveled in the delights of each other. It seemed that they found a new dimension of sensual potency. Tom kissed Lea on many places of her lovely body. Lea purred with pleasure.

Lea responded with abandon, crouching over him like a panther ready to devour him. She kissed his face, his lips and moved up to dangle her pendant breasts over his face. He eagerly took them into his mouth. Quietly moaning with pleasure, she slid down his body kissing as she went. He groaned with pleasure. Her tongue and lips caressed him into a near frenzy of passion. Her sensuous desire grew as she ignited his flesh.

It was exhilarating to Lea to feel his increasing pleasure. As he shivered and stiffened with delight she slowly rolled to his side, and he rose above her. Their heightened passion quickly came to a climax as they loved, and loved, and loved.

They awakened early in the morning strong and vibrant. They quickly dressed and walked to the beach just as the sun was rising from the sea on the eastern horizon. A distant sailboat crossed in front of the sun, painting a beautiful picture. Hand in hand they walked on the hard packed sand that the receding tide had formed.

"Last night was lovely, my dear. It was, how do I say it, the best, the most exquisite love ever," Lea said.

"Not only exquisite, also tantalizing and sensuous. I love you," he replied.

"I love you so much. I'm overflowing with love."

After twenty minutes of strolling the beach they returned to the Patch for breakfast. While waiting they strolled the back lawn and swung to and fro in the hammock and the double swing. A walk on the dock was rewarded by seeing the jumping mullet.

Breakfast was a sumptuous baked, stuffed French toast, with orange juice, fruit and coffee. Andrea's husband, Arthur, and co–innkeeper, carried on a titillating conversation as they enjoyed the breakfast.

After packing and saying good–byes to Andrea and Arthur Mellon, they went to the park across the street to visit the UDT Seal Museum, birthplace of the Navy Frogmen. It was here that formalized training of these underwater demolition teams had begun in 1943.

They drove home after this exciting, lovely engagement honeymoon.

CHAPTER TWENTY NINE

The wind velocity reached sixty knots as tropical storm Alicia built up strength in the Atlantic Ocean east of Florida. The latest forecast on the weather channel warned that Alicia was a large, strong storm and would increase in intensity. The eye of Alicia was five hundred miles east of Florida on a westerly heading. It was forecast to accelerate in velocity reaching hurricane strength, seventy–four knots in twenty–four hours. Moving west at a speed of fifteen miles per hour, landfall was expected in thirty hours. The broadcaster reminded listeners that hurricanes were fickle and unpredictable. Conditions might change. A hurricane warning was posted from the Keys to Cape Canaveral.

Tom was at his computer working on his collection of short stories. The telephone rang. Lea, busy with her crocheting, leaned toward the phone and picked it up.

"Kelley residence. Lea speaking." She listened for a few seconds and called out, "Tom, Helen Masters of the Red Cross for you."

Tom shut down the computer, not forgetting to save his work. "Tom here. Hello Helen."

"I presume you're up to date on Alicia. Am I right?"

"Oh yes. I keep watching the weather channel."

"The projected path of Alicia brings it ashore just South of us about fifty miles. Of course that could change. Anyway, we're opening shelters including yours tomorrow morning at eight o'clock. Can you and Lea be available?"

"Yes, of course. We're ready"

"Fine. The school principal and the janitor will be at the shelter before eight. I'm calling your other people to alert them. Call our head-quarters when you're set–up and ready. Good luck."

"Okay Helen. We'll do our best."

Tom was shelter manager for the county Red Cross unit. Lea was assigned as nurse. Their shelter was a school building two miles from home. The gymnasium, two adjoining rooms and the cafeteria were used as the shelter. This was to be their first test in a real emergency.

"We open our shelter tomorrow at eight in the morning. Alicia is headed toward us." Tom said to Lea.

"I'll check our emergency supply box."

"Okay. I'll get my Red Cross forms and supplies ready, and my two signs that direct people to the shelter. Then I'll bring our things in from the pool deck and the porch."

"Let's get a good night's sleep. We may have sleepless nights ahead of us," Lea added.

Alicia was charging toward the Florida coast. Hurricane force winds were pummeling the coast and inland as far as Tom's shelter. Ninety people came to the shelter and others were making their way through the seventy–five knot wind. Tom called Red Cross headquarters with his hourly report. The eye of the storm was plotted to come ashore near Palm Beach, fifty miles south of Port St. Lucie where the shelter was located. Wind velocity was forecast to be ninety to one hundred knots.

So far, Lea had only minor aches and pains to attend to with the evacuees. Tom enlisted help to operate the shelter from cooperative refugees. Each person could have a three by seven foot space. Some opted to stay in the cafeteria and not claim a floor space. Some people did not come prepared with blankets, snacks and other essentials. One elderly lady staked out a personal territorial space of ten by ten feet. One of Tom's assistants came to Tom for help. He couldn't convince the lady to reduce her space.

"Madam, I'm pleased to see that you came prepared with blankets and personal items," Tom greeted the lady. "The ferocity of the storm means that soon we will be crowded in here. We must be able to accommodate all who seek refuge. To do that, we have to limit the space each person has. Surely you would want all people to be safe from the storm. Please assemble your things in a space of about three by seven feet. You'll not only please me but many other people."

"All right. I didn't realize we'd have so many people," the lady said sheepishly.

As they walked away from her, Tom advised John, his helper, "You see, it's all in how you present the problem."

"You sure did it right. The old lady seemed embarrassed."

Tom went back to his primary job at the entrance of the shelter registering incoming people. As he sat down, the door burst open. A woman screamed, "Help. Please, we need help out here."

Tom bounded out of his chair and raced to the door. He pushed the door closed quickly and faced the now ninety knot wind.

A woman yelled in his ear. "My sister lost her grip on her six year old son. He's being blown across the lawn. He can't get up on his feet. Over there." She pointed in the direction of the flagpole.

Tom said nothing and fought his way through the ferocious wind toward the boy. The child was being rolled along the ground by the wind.

At the moment the rain had subsided into a drizzle, but the ground was soggy. Tom crouched low as he ran toward the boy. Running with the wind Tom quickly closed the distance between himself and the lad. As he neared the child Tom heard him yelling, "Mommy, Mommy" as the wind pushed him as easily as a bulldozer pushed a pile of dirt.

The boy was being blown toward a low brick wall that surrounded the flagpole. He'd be injured if he struck the wall. Tom dove headfirst into the mud and caught one of the lad's legs. They stopped sliding on the mushy ground three feet from the wall. Tom leaned over the child to protect him from blowing debris and saw only scratches and bruises on his face and arms. The boy was crying and hung on to Tom tightly.

Tom cradled him in his arms and fought against the wind toward the shelter. He turned his back to the wind as small branches and other debris pummeled him. They reached the door wet and muddy. The mother was there and took her son. Someone held the door open and they entered the safety of the shelter.

Lea took the boy and treated his scratches and bruises and cleaned some of the mud off him. "Do you have dry clothes for your son?" Lea asked the mother.

"Yes. I'll take him now. Thank you Mr. Kelley and you, Mrs. Kelley."

Lea turned to Tom. "You need a shower and a change of clothes."

"Sure do," Tom said as he turned to James, his assistant manager. "Take over Jim. I'm going to get an hour of rest after cleaning up."

There were now two hundred and sixty-five evacuees in the shelter. Alicia's eye had come ashore about ten miles north of Palm Beach. The shelter was on the edge of the eye, so there might be a period of calm before the wind howled again from the opposite direction. Wind velocity at the shelter had reached one hundred knots. The silent calm of the eye arrived. There was an eerie absence of sound after so much noisy wind.

Jim picked up the public address microphone. "We're in the eye of the storm now folks. Do not leave. As you know the other side of Alicia will arrive soon with more hurricane force wind. Settle down and get some rest if you can. We've still got a few hours of high wind coming."

Tom returned to the gymnasium after his rest. He turned to Lea. "It's time for you to get some rest. If we have a medical emergency we'll wake you."

"Right. I need a break. Is it fairly quiet in that little room where we put our blankets?"

"Yes. You won't hear much of the kids noise coming from the gymnasium. Jim, has it been uneventful while I slept?"

"Yes. No big problems and the people are well behaved."

At about four o'clock in the morning there was a loud crashing noise in the direction of the cafeteria. Tom knew it wasn't just dishes breaking. He and Jim ran to the cafeteria. In a corner of the big room, they saw broken glass and bent window frames. Part of a large tree limb projected into the room. Obviously a large pine tree had been blown down and hit the building. The lights were still on so the tree had not hit a power line. Howling, sometimes screeching wind tore at the silence of the room. As Tom surveyed the damage the school janitor appeared. Tom said, "Fortunately no one was sitting here. What can we do to close up this hole in the building? The wind coming in here will make the cafeteria miserable."

Henry, the janitor, looked over the damage. "I have some canvas tarps that we can put there. I'll need some help putting them up and bracing them against the wind."

"Jim," Tom said. "Go get some volunteers. I'll get on the P–A system."

Tom rushed back to the microphone. "We're okay folks. A pine tree blew down and broke windows in the cafeteria. We'll have the hole closed up with canvas soon. It's windy in there so please refrain from going to the cafeteria until further notice."

Lea came running to Tom. The loud noise had awakened her. Tom told her what had happened and that no injuries had occurred.

The local television station was still broadcasting. The latest report advised that Alicia was now inland and starting to break up. Locally, wind velocity was down to eighty–five knots. Rain had caused isolated minor flooding. Power lines and trees were down from Stuart to West Palm Beach. People were advised to stay in their homes or shelters until further notice.

Tom leaned back and thanked the Almighty. They were nearly through this awful hurricane. No dire emergencies had occurred. The people in the shelter had been cooperative. None were hurt. Lea was bearing up under the strain. The cafeteria crew had kept hot coffee, milk and sandwiches available. The children had been reasonably quiet. Thank goodness they had electrical power all the time.

Tom browsed through the registration forms. Some of the evacuees had come from mobile homes from as far away as Fort Lauderdale. Others stopped their travel on I–95 and the Turnpike to seek shelter.

As dawn lighted the sky Tom went outside to check on the weather The wind was subsiding but still too strong. The parking lot was flooded with two inches of water and he could see the tree that had come down on the cafeteria. The big trunk of the tree lay against the corner of the building. The sign at the driveway had blown away. But it was reassuring to see a trace of sunshine in the east.

Two hours later the television reporter advised that winds were down to fifty–five knots. Tom called Red Cross headquarters with one of his hourly reports. "Two hundred sixty–five evacuees here. No injuries. Minor damage to the building. Food supply adequate for six more hours. How soon can you give the all clear?"

Helen answered. "It's almost over Tom. Wind is down to fifty. You'll get the all clear within the hour. We'll have a critique meeting tomorrow at ten in the morning. Bring your reports. Thank you and Lea for a job well done."

Tom briefed the evacuees. Some of them wanted to leave the shelter immediately. Tom told them he had no authority to keep them there, but advised them to stay until the all clear was given. A few people gathered up their belongings and left. Most, still wary and frightened by the hurricane, stayed.

In about an hour the all clear was given. The people left and sloshed through the water to their cars.

At noon Tom and Lea packed their emergency supplies, thanked all the helpers who were still there, and went home.

Their home had survived without a scratch. Small debris littered the lawn. Without unpacking, they collapsed on the bed for a much needed rest.

CHAPTER THIRTY

In June they were married. It was a grand affair. Sons, daughters, grand children and friends were invited to come to the wedding on a river boat. They cruised down the Indian River and were married by the captain. The reception dinner was held at a local restaurant in a private room for thirty guests. Tom kept a small secret from Lea. As they walked down the dock from the boat, there waiting for them was a big limousine. Lea said, "I wonder who's riding in that big limo?"

"Guess," Tom said proudly.

"Us?"

"Of course."

"You' re so unpredictable and nice."

With four grandchildren they traveled in style to the Admiral's Table restaurant and the gala dinner celebration. Toasts, laughter and unbridled happiness overwhelmed the bride and groom. Pictures by the dozens were taken. Then, as the guests finished their dessert, Tom announced, "Find your way home good friends. Lea and I are leaving." He raised his glass and quietly toasted, "A votre sante."

They spent a one night honeymoon in an elegant hotel room on the eighth floor of a hotel on the beach. Their room overlooked the ocean. A little after sunrise Lea awoke and carefully slipped out of bed. She didn't want to wake Tom. She went to the large windows overlooking the ocean and gazed contentedly at the beautiful morning. As she stood there, a flock of nine pelicans cruised slowly by the window, their V–formation perfect. What a wonderful sight, Lea thought. What a lucky woman I am. Here I am in a paradise with the man I love.

She crawled back in bed and put an arm around Tom. She wanted him to wake up. She wanted more of his love. Again, they entwined exploring more of each other's body. Their passion was overwhelming. They reached the precipice of sexual desire and fell into the abyss of exhaustion.

CHAPTER THIRTY ONE

"Let's go, Miss Priss," Tom called Lea's nickname as she came out of the bedroom.

"Yes sir colonel. But I'm wearing the star pendant you gave me. Doesn't that mean that I outrank you?"

"Oh. Yes sir, General Priss. I mean General Kelley. Hurry or we'll be late."

They were going to the local County airport to watch an airshow. After a thirty minute drive they were there in time to see an old P–51 fighter do a low–level roll past the control tower.

"Wow, that's a beautiful airplane," Lea exclaimed.

"Yes. Sure is. That's one we had in Europe way back in the dark ages."

They prowled around inside an old B–24 bomber that was on display. A flight of four modern Air Force Jets did their aerobatics, trailing colored smoke. An old bi–wing Waco airplane did his thing roaring over the crowd. Then the local light aircraft pilots did a flyby—a mixture of Pipers, a Beechcraft, a Cessna and other small planes.

Tom pointed out the Cessna to Lea. "There's one like I was in when I had a *hairy* experience. It happened in Texas. But enough of my stories. It's time for me to hear one of your memories. Come, let's go to the coffee shop for a snack and perhaps you'd tell me a fascinating story."

As they ordered their coffee Lea started. "One of the fondest memories of my early married life involves my three children. The children were eight, twelve and fourteen years old. About four years ago I drove to a site that brought back those happy memories. I saw the words Euclid Beach Park. Built 1895. As I passed through the arched entrance, I saw the old gray stone towers on each side. Yellow, ragged flags at the top of each tower still waved in the summer breeze. This was once the entrance to the number one amusement park in Cleveland, Ohio. Now, it was old and drab. As I drove over the rutted road leading to the sandy beaches of Lake Erie, I remembered the fun I had with my children in this park."

T.J. asked, "Those were the good old days, right?"

"Yes. There were mobile homes neatly lined in rows along the beach. In the old days this was the location of the tracks and hills of the 'Thriller,' the highest, steepest roller–coaster in the country. Around a curve in the road I saw my favorite spot, the buckeye tree, standing tall and stately with large branches spreading over a sandy area of beach. I parked the car under the tree and walked toward the shore. The waves were gently breaking on the shore. It was still serene after all these years. The sun reflected across the water producing a golden path from shore to horizon. I sat down under the buckeye tree and closed my eyes, letting my mind drift back.

"I remembered preparing a picnic lunch and placing it in a yellow wicker basket. We would feast on Keftethakia (meatballs), tomatoes, black Greek olives, feta cheese and crusty French bread. Homemade Karithata (pecan crescents) and honeydew melon would top off the picnic.

"At eight o'clock in the morning we piled into the car for the ride to the beach. There was magic in the air as we heard the roar of the coasters and the screaming of the riders as we approached the park.

"The aroma of popcorn and cotton candy filled the air. Our mouths watered at the thought of these delicacies. We loved all the rides but nothing compared to the Thriller. We would race to it first. The line was long so we bought frozen custard in a honey cone while waiting. Finally it was our turn to ride. As we jumped into the front seat, the bar would lock to keep us from falling out. The smell of machine oil came up from the tracks. Slowly the car chugged up the hill, creaking on the tracks. We all squeezed the bar tightly. Looking down I saw the wooden lattice frame vibrate. 'Hang on tight, kids,' I shouted. The spectators on the ground became smaller as we climbed higher and higher. I held my breath as the car approached the peak of the highest hill. At the top the car hesitated for a moment. Everyone was quiet as I looked down the steep hill. Suddenly the Thriller moved forward. The car became almost vertical as it plunged down. Terrified screams could be heard all the way down. The wind blew everyone's hair straight back and took our breaths away. My stomach did flip–flops as I looked at the children. They were yelling and screaming but enjoying every minute of the ride. Then came the 180 degree turn swaying us to the right and making the ride very bumpy. The finale was just as spectacular with four small hills which seemed to almost eject us out of the car. What a thrill for three minutes.

"I try to blot out the bad times of later years. Now, the wonderful years of *September Song* fill me with gratitude for you and my life with you."

"I'm glad you told me this story," Tom said. "It's good to know that there were happy times in your life. I hope there were more happy times than bad times."

"But now, what's your story about a scary experience in a Cessna?"

"Okay. But to get across the full impact of the event I want you to imagine that you're with me in the Cessna. It's a four–place aircraft and there were only three of us in it. Picture yourself in the back seat with me.

"Nacadoches is the name of the small town in East Texas. It was a hot, miserable day in the summer of 1956.

"Our mobile radar station was set up there during a maneuvers training exercise to test the air defense around that area. After setting up radar and radio equipment, we waited for the aircraft to come over so we could track them. Waiting and more waiting. That was the name of the game. The wretched, sweating soldiers who sat in the hot, dark tents watching the radar screens were nearly the only ones actively doing something constructive.

"Jake and I strolled around checking equipment, trying to look serious and official, while bitching about the heat. We strolled over to the operations room of the tiny airfield with its four thousand foot runway.

"We went in, closing the door quickly because the room was air–conditioned by a wheezing window unit. George, the airport manager, chuckled, 'You guys sure look like the dregs of Hades. Want a cold one?'

'Sure do. Why else would we be in this rat trap?' Jake replied.

George said excitedly, 'There's a hangar party up in Longview about seventy miles North tonight. Wanna go?'

"Jake and I knew about hangar parties. Lots of beer, whiskey, girls, dancing and fun. We looked at each other with a nod of heads, knowing we could get someone else to pull the duty tonight.

"I said elatedly, 'Sure. Are you flying your Cessna?'

"'Yep. We leave at seven–thirty.'

"At seven–thirty that evening we walked over to where George was warming up the Cessna and climbed aboard. Jake took the right front seat and I climbed into the back seat.

"George ran up the engine, checked the gauges, and off we went on the short flight.

"At Longview there were many light aircraft of all types. Most were there for the party. It was all as advertised—dancing in a big hangar, lots of booze, and a bevy of attractive East Texas girls. We had a ball.

"At about eleven–thirty George swayed over to us, slightly under the weather from drinking his favorite bourbon and muttered, 'Let's go. I've got a busy day tomorrow.'

"'You okay to fly, George?' Jake said apprehensively.

"'Sure.'

"We raced down the runway and pulled up into the black night sky. A high overcast obscured the moon and stars. George flew by visual flight rules, not instruments. He knew this area like the back of his hand. The city and village lights told him where we were. Flying at five thousand feet, we approached Nacadoches, and George started the final approach. He pulled up suddenly and shouted, 'This ain't Nacadoches. There's two runways down there. Naco has only one.'

"Jake and I looked down and saw only one runway. Jake exasperatedly said, 'George, the bourbon is giving you two runways. It's Naco all right. There's only one runway.'

"Jake and I knew what to do. Our first job as aircraft controllers was to exude calm and confidence, and transmit it to George.

"I quickly said, 'You're the pilot so you have to land the airplane. Here's what we'll do. Jake'll talk you down just like ground control approach radar would do. Which of your eyes is the better one?'

"George simpered, 'right one.'

'Okay. Turn starboard and go around. How much fuel do you have?'

"George looked at the gauges and hesitantly figured, 'forty–five *gallums*, about nine minutes of flying, I calculate.'

'Okay. Jake take over. Get us on the runway.'

"Jake sat up straight peering through the windscreen. 'George, pick out the right hand runway and fly down to it, I'll correct you as needed. If you're missing it, I'll yell pull up. Do it immediately and go around. We'll have enough fuel for a second try but that has to be a good one.'

"You're sinking too fast, George. Add some power. That's good. When we get closer, I'll be able to tell how good the approach is. Fly the instruments. Don't look outside. Five degrees left. Hold your airspeed. Pull up now!' Jake yelled.

"George was still alert enough to follow orders and banked right while climbing. We skimmed the tops of the pine trees near the end of the runway.

"Jake calmly advised, 'We were a little long. You're doin' fine George. Make a wide right turn now. Level off. Keep the wings level. Look at the instruments. Airspeed is good.'

"As Jake was getting us lined up properly, I could see George sweating. He was concentrating on the instruments and I figured we'd make it.

"'Start your descent,' Jake advised. 'You're on final approach now. You're at eight hundred feet. Ten degrees left. Decrease power a little. Come back right five degrees. Three hundred feet. Sinking too fast. Add power. That's enough. Disregard the runway lights. Look at your instruments. I'm putting you down. Okay, reduce power. Flare out now. You're fifty feet over the end of the runway. Let her sink slowly. Pull up the nose a little. Reduce power. Level off. You'll touch down in seconds. Nice, George. There's the touch down, all three wheels. Chop the power. Stand on the brakes. We're a little long. More brakes, George.'

"We squealed to a stop ten feet from the end of the runway. George, sweating profusely, collapsed against the steering column. Jake and I sat there motionless, saying nothing for a full minute. We got out of the Cessna and sat on the runway leaving George in the cockpit. We looked at each other and simultaneously said, 'Never again with George.'"

CHAPTER THIRTY TWO

The 'Red Tail Hawk' was the name of the restaurant where Tom and Lea went to dinner. It was located on the beach overlooking the ocean. A huge live oak tree spread its limbs over part of the building and shaded the entrance. A wood slatted walkway wound its way through the sea grape all around the building. They ambled slowly along the walk listening to the night sounds. They paused to look at the ocean. A gentle surf caressed the sandy shore and as it receded, drew grains of sand with it. As if the ocean needed sand for nourishment, the ebbing tide kept devouring the beach grain by grain. Of course, with the incoming tide, a few grains would be given back. The soft summer wind came serenely through the sea grape leaves rustling them gently. On the horizon, out on the sea, the sparkling lights of a cruise ship announced to shore–bound people, "sorry you are not with us you poor landlubbers."

It was so beautiful and peaceful that Tom and Lea could hardly draw themselves away to have dinner.

"Come, we've soaked up enough of this paradise. Let's have dinner," Lea pleaded.

"You spoil–sport. How can you leave this gorgeous view, this surf, this cool breeze, just because you're hungry? Come to think of it, you're right. I'm hungry too."

Their table was at the windows overlooking the ocean. A more idyllic setting for a lovely dinner could not be found. As Lea set her wine glass down and gazed into Tom's eyes she murmured softly, "T.J. I hope you agree with my latest *brilliant* idea. You've had some wine. Perhaps you'll be in a receptive mood. Sometime soon, I'd like for us to make a trip on AMTRAK along the trek on the Lake Shore Limited between Cleveland and Chicago. I want to reminisce and relive our meeting. It would be marvelous."

Immediately he raised his wine glass and chanted, "To the lady whose mind whirls in the same orbit at the same time as mine. I've been thinking the same thing." Their glasses clicked, their eyes poured forth love.

"Let's dance, T.J. This trio sounds good and they are playing 'In the Mood.'"

"Yes, and I'll request September Song."

As they danced to the slow dreamy music, they quietly talked of their AMTRAK trip.

"You know how I like to travel and see new places. And as you've said before, remembering is a wonderful thing, the essence of life." Lea said.

"While we're in upstate New York I'd like to visit a cousin of mine who lives near Syracuse."

"Fine with me, Tom. Let's go home now. I'm tired."

CHAPTER THIRTY THREE

It was one week before they were to leave for England and France, June 1, 1994. The sparkle of the moonlight on the surface of the pool was broken into ripples by the two swimmers. Lea detached herself from Tom and with a smooth backstroke broke free of the entanglement. From the middle of the pool she said, "If we don't quit this fooling around we'll soon be in the house in a prone position. Maybe even here on the deck or on the porch."

"Nothing wrong with that, love. And any position is fine with me."

"You rascal. Not yet, later," she said seductively. "Come on. You get out first and hold a towel for me when I get out."

They had been skinny–dipping for twenty minutes. When they left the pool the hoard of glistening diamonds returned to the surface of the pool. They relaxed in the padded chaise–lounges and absorbed the beauty of the night.

They thanked God for bringing them together.

Lea sighed, "I'd like to tell you some of the innermost, private thoughts I had about four years ago. That was just after I had come down here to see you. The first time we had seen each other since meeting on the Lake Shore Limited. I was back in Cleveland thinking about us. I couldn't get you out of my mind. An uncontrollable yearning for you occupied my mind. You inspired me in different ways. I dared to be different, to be adventurous, as you put it. Your innermost thoughts written in your letters inspired me to have new courageous thoughts about us together. I remember going to one of your favorite restaurants. The one on the beach overlooking the ocean. It was a beautiful evening and I felt like a school girl on her first date. I think I knew then, deep in my heart, that we were meant for each other. I love you."

"I too felt like a nervous school boy on his first date when I met you at the airport with bells on," Tom admitted.

"I love you." Come on you old reprobate. Let's go inside. I want to show you how much I love you."

"Wait," Tom said. "Look at the sky. No moon, it's very dark, all other people have retired. Here, under the oak tree, on the deck, on the chaise cushions is the love nest for tonight. No one will see us. Just think how romantic we can be."

"It would be nice, different and adventurous. Yes. Let's do it."

Their love making was tender and frenzied. They explored new vistas of romance.

CHAPTER THIRTY FOUR

At the British Air ticket counter in Miami Tom and Lea presented their tickets and passports to the young lady clerk. They were both dressed nicely, Tom in a light blue sport jacket, navy blue pants and white broad–brim hat. Lea was beautiful in a light blue dress and white hat.

The clerk smiled. "(You two look so nice, as we British say, 'dressed to the nines', we are going to move you up to Club Class seats. Would that be acceptable?"

Tom and Lea glanced at each other and in unison smiled saying, "Of course. Thank you."

The flight was smooth, the service excellent as was the food and they dozed contentedly in their roomy seats. They landed at Heathrow airport on time, passed through customs and boarded a bus to their hotel. As the bus arrived at the front of the hotel, Tom stopped at the entrance and grabbed Lea's arm. "Lea, look at the name of the hotel, Kensington Palace, and there's Hyde Park across the street. This is where I was in early 1944. Then the hotel was called Kensington Gardens Mansion. It must have been bombed after I left. This is a new hotel on the site of the old one."

"Really. You think this is the place where you had the, shall I say, interlude with the flight nurse?"

"It must be. Right across the street, there in Hyde Park, is where the bomb exploded. I can't believe this. Unexpectedly revisiting a memorable site of my life long ago."

Their stay in England was brief. The next day they saw Windsor Castle, Buckingham Palace, Westminster Abbey and Big Ben, the bus making quick stops for picture taking. In the evening they saw a zany comedy called "Run For Your Wife".

On June 3rd they traveled to Southampton. They saw the Bargate which dates back to Norman times, and Pilgrims Tower commemorating the sailing of the Mayflower in 1620. They boarded a ferry for the four and a half hour voyage across the English channel to Cherbourg, France.

Halfway across Lea said, "I need a dramamine. This is a rough trip. My tummy is churning. Would you get me some water, Tom?"

"Sure thing, Miss Priss. Got to have you in good shape when we get to Normandy. This is a smooth crossing compared to D–Day."

"You're a good sailor you hardy soul."

On the bus to their hotel in Caen they stopped briefly at St. Mere Eglise. Tom explained, "This is the village where one of our paratroopers got hung up on a spire of the church. There it is. The paratrooper watched as his buddies below were killed by the Nazis."

"How awful. Did he survive?"

"Yes."

They arrived at their hotel, the Holiday Inn City Centre in Caen at five in the afternoon. The next day would start early at seven o'clock. Their tour bus left at eight o'clock for a visit to a D–Day Museum in Arromanche and the ruins of German coastal guns and bunkers at the town of Longue. Lunch was in Bayeaux at the Salen De Le Quick Lunch where they had soup, pizza and hot chocolate for 134 francs. Tom hesitantly tried his French. "Vous avez un beau restaurant ici et nous enjoy tres bon. Merci."

"What does that mean?" Lea asked.

"In broken French, 'You have a good restaurant here and we enjoy it very much. Thank you.'"

A visit to the Cathedral of Notre Dame in Bayeaux was inspiring. The cathedral dated back to the year 1077. Lea took video pictures and Tom manned the snapshot camera.

That evening in the lounge they each ordered a brandy alexander. Fortunately Pierre Salinger was there and explained in French to the bartender how to mix the drink. They had a nice chat with Mr. Salinger for twenty minutes.

The next day they went to the American cemetery at Colleville sur Mer. This cemetery, where over 9,000 American boys are buried, is on the high ground behind the beach where the American troops invaded Normandy. At the edge of the one hundred foot bluff overlooking the beach, they could see Vierville sur Mer where Tom had landed in 1944.

Tom remembered the horror of that day. Again, he saw the dead American lying face down at the water edge, and the shell hole half filled with water with a hand stretched toward the sky out of the water. He saw the defile where a soldier ahead of him stepped on a land mine. These memories tugged at his heart. Lea stepped back and silently let Tom relive the days of fifty years ago. She took a photo of Tom, the beach and Vierville sur Mer. Later, when the film was developed, the grim look on Tom's face "said it all", as Lea's sister remarked.

On June 6th, the anniversary day, they attended the memorial ceremony on Omaha Beach at Colleville sur Mer. Bands from several countries marched and played. Old World War II aircraft flew overhead. The pomp and pageantry was impressive. Tom said, "I know what's coming next and I don't think I'd like to stay for it. The heads of State will give their canned speeches saying what the mass of people want to hear. Their speech writers will have included the necessary platitudes. I know, that's quite cynical, but that's how I feel. Come, let's walk back up the road to a little sidewalk cafe we passed."

"If that's what you want, sure," she agreed.

"Maybe I'll find an elderly Frenchman who was here on D–Day. It would be more interesting to try to talk with him or a woman who was here then."

After almost two hours at the cafe and not making contact with a Frenchman who spoke English, they rejoined their tour group for the ride back to the hotel.

The next day they traveled to the village of Saint Jamesin Brittany where over four thousand Americans are buried. Row up row of white crosses were lined up perfectly. After a brief ceremony honoring the soldiers who gave their lives, taps was sounded with an echo sound that was emotionally wrenching for Tom. His eyes welled with tears.

The village had brought two groups of school children to the cemetery. Tom approached the leader of a group of children. He had heard her speaking English. "Pardon me madam. Why are so many children here?"

"Mon ami, we teach the children the history of D–Day and how you Americans fought the Nazis to liberate us. They learn to appreciate your sacrifices as we adults do."

"Thank you. I am pleased to hear that you do this."

"Also monsieur, the children help tending the graves in order to keep the cemetery looking nice."

"Ah, marvelous. I wish we taught our children about the significance of D–Day. Merci," Tom said.

The tour then went to the nearby town of Avranches. As they arrived, the streets were lined with local town folks, all waving and shouting "Merci" to the veterans. After parking the buses they walked three blocks to the town square and city hall. All along the way Tom shook hands with the people and graciously accepted their thanks saying, "Bon jour, et merci a vous aussi." At the town square, the mayor gave a speech and presented medals to some of the veterans. A United States Navy band played big band music of the forties era. Tom danced with Lea and with some of the town ladies. He signed about twenty autographs for children including his name on a balloon. As is the French custom, Tom kissed the ladies and some men on both cheeks twice. After tasting the local wine, Tom and Lea left at six o'clock.

"It's very gratifying to know that the French people still appreciate what we did for them," Tom said.

The following day early in the morning they visited the Battle of Normandy Museum in Caen. Tom 's name was in the log book and on a temporary Wall of Liberty display. The permanent Wall would be in the garden just recently finished. They watched a movie of different aspects of the invasion displayed on three screens simultaneously.

In the afternoon they returned to Colleville sur Mer for a special ceremony for D–Day veterans. Six veterans including Tom who landed on Omaha beach were presented with a commemorative French medal and given certificates making them honorary citizens of the villages of Colleville sur Mer, St. Laurent and Vierville sur Mer. Wine and cookies were served in the little town hall. It came to mind again, how grateful and sincere these people were, especially the older ones who had lived through the occupation and the liberation.

They were back at their hotel early. The festivities in Normandy were finished and the next day they went to Paris. Sightseeing from the bus included the Eiffel Tower, Notre Dame, the Louvre the Opera House and Tom's favorite cafe. "There's the Cafe de le Pais. I was there in forty–four and again in forty–five."

"What's the big attraction there?" she asked.

"They say, you will always meet a friend there. Everyone eventually goes to this cafe."

They arrived at the Hotel Mercure in the afternoon. That evening at the Paradis Latin, a dinner night club, Lea and T.J. sat at a table on a side balcony. The dinner of filet mignon, four side dishes and baked Alaska was superb. The floor show included a trapeze act that swung to and fro in front of them at eye level. On the stage, bare–breasted beautiful chorus girls pranced and danced. It was a delightful evening.

As they left the *boite de nui*, Tom asked the doorman to get a taxi. Tom tipped the doorman and they entered the taxi. They glanced at the meter as the driver pulled away from the curb. The meter already read twenty–one francs.

"Look T. J., we're charged twenty–one francs before we even start."

"That's ridiculous. Driver, why does your meter read twenty–one francs so soon?"

In broken English the aged driver said, "It is standard charge."

"It's too much," Lea argued.

"Allez. Go. Allez," the driver said sharply as he pulled over to the curb.

"Merci, mon ami," T.J. said icily.

As they stood there three blocks from the Paradis Latin they looked at each other with consternation.

"Maybe all taxis are like that," Lea bristled.

"Let's get a taxi ourselves. We'll see."

Two blocks farther down the street they were successful in hailing a cab. Entering the cab they saw, with dismay, the same driver and the same twenty–one francs. At the same time he noticed who they were.

"Allez. Allez."

"Gladly monsieur," Lea hissed.

Tired and frustrated, they looked at each other and burst out laughing. They regained their composure and T.J. said, "Can you believe it? We picked the same taxi, the same old ogre of a driver. As my friend, Jules, would say, 'Our cups runneth under'. We are so unlucky."

"Gay Paree, the city of light. I wish we were back in Normandy where the people are polite and appreciate us Americans," Lea said.

"You're so right. Come. We have to try again. Let's walk three or four blocks and get away from the demon of Paris," Tom suggested.

"We'd better get one soon, I'm tired."

Ten minutes later they stopped another taxi. Their first glance was at the meter. It showed eleven francs.

"Good enough for me," Tom muttered.

"Me too," Lea concurred.

On the way to the hotel Tom was able to converse, sparingly in French, with the driver. He was pleasant and polite. They joked with each other and understood each other's fractured phrases.

Upon arrival, T.J. tipped him generously and happily said, "Merci mon ami. Vous are le best de tout le drivers."

Scheduled for the next day was a trip to the Palace at Versailles. Lea videotaped it all—the beautiful painted ceilings, statuary, the hall of mirrors, Queen Antoinette's bedroom, the garden and a room commemorating Napoleon s battles. The opulence of the era was captured on Lea's film.

Back to the hotel to await the piece de resistance of the day, a dinner cruise on the Seine River. It was a huge boat, brightly lit with colored lights, superb service, a strolling accordion player, and the most delicious and opulent dinner ever. Wine and champagne flowed freely. The filet mignon was the most tender they had ever tasted. Lobster tail, tossed salad, green beans, scalloped potatoes and baked Alaska were excellent. Lea and Tom danced on board the boat. After this wonderful evening they returned to the hotel to get ready for the flight home the next day.

"Lea dear, the city of light would be more aptly named the city of love. My love for you is overflowing from within me. I'm in an especially romantic mood tonight. Could I entice you to, you know, etcetera, etcetera."

"You don't have to entice me to make love. I too feel romantic, the urge. I'm ready."

At Charles DeGaulle airport they went through customs twice. One of the agents hesitated when he saw the two bottles of special vintage wine labeled "For the Fiftieth Anniversary of Liberation."

"Monsieur, these rare bottles of wine must be very expensive. They will require an export tax." At this point he looked up and saw Tom's American D–Day badge. "Pardon, mon ami. For you, a liberator, there is no charge. Please pass on."

"Merci." Tom smiled.

The other agent, hearing this conversation asked, "Monsieur, would you please autograph my liberation book?"

"Oui, of course. I am happy to do this."

"Merci, merci."

Finally they flew across the ocean to JFK airport, then down to Miami, arriving home very tired but happy with their trip to the 50th.

CHAPTER THIRTY FIVE

The Silver Meteor AMTRAK train rumbled into the station at West Palm Beach, Florida only four minutes late. Lea and Tom were waiting at their assigned position on the platform. They were going on their trip to upstate New York for two or three days in the area where Tom grew up, and to a little village named McDonough. In the 20s and 30s Tom's family visited relatives and friends there. Then, they'd continue on the Lake Shore Limited to Cleveland.

It was a sunny, warm day and their spirits were soaring as they boarded the train. The attendant was very attentive and showed them how the facilities of the room operated. Upper and lower bunks folded out and there was a sink and toilet in the small cramped space. It was suitable and they were happy to be on their trip—eight thousand miles throughout the country. "Board," the conductor shouted. In today's fast–paced, frenetic world they no longer shout "All Aboard," as if the three tenths of a second saved by eliminating "All" would help keep the train on time. Lea and Tom settled down in their little compartment to enjoy the scenery.

The rough track bed in North Florida caused their car to sway and bounce. On into the Carolinas they sped, passing small villages where the trains stopped in days of old, but now were by–passed. It became a challenge to try to see the names of the villages on the old abandoned train stations as they roared by. Quaint old houses desperately needing paint, tobacco drying sheds, dirt roads disappearing into the woods quickly faded away. In the villages, small children waved to the train. Tom and Lea waved back. Graffiti covered some of the old warehouse walls. One pronounced "Winos and children shall rule the earth."

They went to the lounge car for cocktails before dinner. There they visited with a seventy–five year old woman who had just lost her husband to cancer. Tom said, "I know how you feel. I lost my first wife to cancer some time ago. It's a difficult time to go through."

At the same table, a sixteen year old girl sat near them. She was on her way to visit her grandmother and a boyfriend who lived nearby. They finished their cocktails, went to dinner in the dining car, and returned to their room. They were awake early the next morning. Tom had endured a restless sleep in the upper bunk while Lea could not get accustomed to the constant swaying of the car.

Tom said, "I can't take the confines of that upper bunk. It gives me claustrophobia. Can I snuggle up to you tomorrow night?"

"It's a pretty narrow bed. We'll be packed in there like sardines. But I'll like it."

The time seemed to pass slowly. They were anxious to get to the next part of their journey on a different train.

After changing trains in New York City, they boarded the Lake Shore Limited. They followed the Hudson River North, skirting the banks of the river. Along the way, the scenery was beautiful but sometimes marred by old, dilapidated buildings. Long unused warehouses, spurs of abandoned railroad track, faded lettering on old business buildings, all spoke of the good days in past years. "I rode these rails way back in thirty–nine, Lea. Went to be with a friend on New Years Eve," Tom said.

"Bet you wowed the young girls and had a ball."

Through the window they saw a small castle built on an island in the river. It was unoccupied and falling into disrepair.

"A railroad baron or some wealthy family long ago probably built the castle as a summer place, away from the confusion of the big city," Tom conjectured.

"Yes, probably one of the robber barons of the late 1800's. What a lovely place it must have been," Lea said.

Onward they journeyed, turning West at Albany, and following another river. Soon they came into Syracuse where they would stay for three days. After a night of peaceful rest in a motel, they rented a car and started their side trip to McDonough, New York.

McDonough was founded in 1816, and had a population of about four hundred. Ken Eccleston, Tom's cousin, lived near the village in a log house he built himself. It wasn't a log cabin, but a large two–story house with attic. Ken's maternal grandmother was a Cherokee Indian while his paternal grandmother was a Mohawk. When Ken was a young boy in the 1920s, his heritage wasn't bragged about. There was still a reserve, even a mistrust of native Americans. Ken, however, had steeped himself in Indian lore as it applied to his family.

Ken, his father Linn, and his grandfather Charlie, all had the same first name of Charlie. Therefore, Ken and Linn used their middle names.

Lea and Tom were greeted heartily by Ken and his wife, Barbara.

"Coffee is brewing. Please, sit here in the kitchen. Lea, I hope you like strong coffee. We like it almost too strong to stir," Barbara advised.

"I'll add water," Lea said smiling.

"The stronger the better," Tom interjected. "I got addicted to strong coffee while building a camp in the woods. Good old boiled in a huge pot with egg shells coffee."

Lea grimaced.

"Ken, tell me more about your life as a youngster. I got your letter telling of you being the no–brakes kid. You must have more fascinating tales to tell. I've got my tape recorder ready. Come on, give me some words of wisdom," Tom asked.

"But I'm only seventy–one years old. How much wisdom can I have?" A hearty laugh went all around the table then Ken started. "When I was about seventeen I started building an airplane on my Dad's farm. It was my own design and I used old farm implements and tractor parts. I had it almost finished except for an engine when World War II came upon us. I left for the army and had duty as an aircraft mechanic. When I returned home I found my airplane in pieces. Dad had used the longerons to prop up the pole beans. Other parts had been used for more farm purposes. But I didn't care. I was through with air-planes."

"A great story Ken." Tom was fascinated.

Ken was wound up now and small fantastic tales came flowing forth.

Tom interrupted. "Wait. I've got to put a new tape in the recorder. And Ken, that Indian name, Geneganslet Lake, reminds me of some-thing. You're pretty well up on Indian lore. Do you know anything of the history of Caughdenoy, a little village near Syracuse. I have a niece who lives near there, and the name fascinates me."

"Ah yes. I just happen to know that one. My Mohawk ancestors on grandmother's side were from that area. Caughdenoy is a very small vil-lage. The name is an Americanization of the Indian name. In Mohawk language it is, 'Te–kah–koon–goon–da–nah–yea.'"

"Wait Ken. Spell that please. That's a tough one."

After the spelling, Ken continued. "It means, place where the eel is lying down. It was a crossing of Indian trails in the woods near the Oneida River. The Indians hunted and fished for eel there. The first white settler in Caughdenoy was Myron Stevens who built his house in 1797. The population was two–hundred in 1895. Besides farming small cleared plots of land, the eel business was profitable for many years. Eel was a delicacy food much sought after.

"Picture it." Ken added. "Two Indian trails crossing in the woods. Imagine the now friendly Mohawks teaching Myron Stevens the attrib-utes of the eel business. As the years flowed by, two–hundred white inhabitants carved out a living farming, logging, and fishing for eels. Today, the population is the same. There's no more logging, no more eels, and very little farming."

"I really enjoy your stories, Ken. It's all fascinating to me. Thanks a lot. If you don't mind, I'll write them and embellish a bit, to make them into "stories". We'd better go now. We have miles to travel and things to do." Tom said.

"Thanks Ken," Lea chimed in. "You've given Tom enough grist for the writer's mill to keep him busy for a while. And Barb, thanks for your hospitality."

"Come visit us any time. You're always welcome," Ken said.

CHAPTER THIRTY SIX

The Lake Shore Limited rushed through western New York State, charging on south of Buffalo, and moving into the vineyards near the little village of Ripley.

"Look at those miles of grape vines. Perhaps the chablis we had last night for dinner was from these vineyards. To me, it tasted as good as French wine," Tom mused.

"Yes. It had just the right tang. I wish we weren't going so fast. Then we could see the grapes hanging on the vines," Lea said.

The sun was setting and through the large window of their compartment Tom and Lea could see the brilliant streams of varied color radiating from the sun through the sparse clouds. Tom was reminded of his previous trip along this route. He looked out at the scenery and the sun and remembered the same trip when he was alone. But these were new glorious days, happy days.

The train and its passengers rushed on into Ohio. Lea and Tom were nearing the objective of this trip—Cleveland and their initial meeting. As the train slowed coming into Cleveland, they looked at each other and an unspoken agreement of what would happen next came to them.

"I'll see you in the lounge car, Tom," Lea smiled.

"Of course. Ten minutes. No more."

Tom ambled through the cars toward the lounge. He paused at the door to the lounge. Lea was at a window with her back to him. Good. He would come to her as a stranger, unexpectedly.

"Good morning. May I sit with you for a cup of coffee?"

Lea paused just as before, then said, "If you like."

"I'm on a long therapeutic journey," Tom advised.

"I'm trying to sort out my life," Lea said.

And so it went, reliving their meeting of long ago. They did not pour their hearts out to each other as before. That was unnecessary and to a degree too morbid. Not with a glass of wine, but with their cups of coffee they toasted each other. To your health. It was charming, fun and reinforced their love as they reviewed the days of their meeting. The rumble of the powerful diesel engine and the slow movement of the train announced the beginning of the end of their quest for remembrance. Tom and Lea sat in silence, contemplating the past, the present, the future. Lea began humming their song. At the appropriate time Tom chimed in with words. They quietly sang.

"It's a long, long time from May 'til December. But the days grow short when you reach September. When the autumn weather turns the leaves to flame, one hasn't got time for the waiting game. Oh, the days dwindle down to a precious few, September, November. And these few precious days I'll spend with you. These precious days I'll spend with you."

Before they knew it, their day–dreaming and recollections had brought them to Chicago. The place where their relationship had been cemented in one second of time. Luggage in hand they left the Lake Shore Limited and entered the huge train station. As they walked quietly into the waiting room with its high ceiling and huge windows, the sun streamed in and seemed to focus on a spot in the middle of the room. As they reached this brightly lighted open space, Tom and Lea stopped and placed their luggage on the floor.

Tom put his arm around Lea's waist and drew her to him. He kissed her very lightly on her softest lips in the world.

"Do you have to rush off to catch your train to Milwaukee?" Lea smiled up at Tom.

Tom in his mellifluous, silver–toned voice answered, "No Lea. These precious days I'll spend with you."